The Paranormal and Normal Investigators

Stephen Rhoades

Cover Design, Cover Art by Betty Rocksteady

E-Book Edition ISBN: 979-8-9894535-9-7

Paperback Edition ISBN: 978-1-967519-01-9

Hardback Edition ISBN: 978-1-967519-00-2

Burial Books LLC
4000 Eagle Point Corporate Drive
Suite 303
Birmingham, AL 35242
www.burialbooks.com

Also by Stephen Rhoades

Anthologies
Inanimate Things: Volume One
Inanimate Things: Volume Two
Weird Tales to Haunt Your Reptilian Brain

Novels
The California Butcher

Part One: Prom

Chapter 1

"Bang! Bang!" Buddy whispered while squinting down the sights on a Glock 19.

He was in his thirties, overweight, and standing behind a tree on one side of a clearing in the forest. His weapon was aimed at a man bathed in bright light and seated prostrate in front of a humongous tree with a huge base. There were two bright yellow beams shining out of the trunk, smothering the canopy with a menacing glow.

Buddy lowered the pistol. He had followed Terrence Wright since just before sunset. The man just had to be responsible for the ten-year-old girl who went missing a few days ago. Buddy didn't have any evidence but that's why he was in the woods...to get some proof.

He hadn't liked the way Terrence talked at the Walmart, or the way his eyes wandered when he passed the girls in the produce section. Sure, Buddy liked to look at girls' butts just as much as anyone, but he wasn't a creep like Terrence. There was just something about the man that screamed child molester, and like many of the great investigators before him, Buddy followed his gut.

That was the first thing Buddy learned as a member of the Security Force. Well that, and if you're gonna shoot somebody, then you better have some proof.

No, wait a minute.

Maybe it was if you're gonna shoot somebody, shoot to kill. Whatever, he couldn't remember those damned rules anyhow.

Franklin Waldrop had never been quite smart enough to remember things like rules and formulas, which was why he never got past the tenth grade. Nobody had called him Franklin for as long as he could remember. Now he was just Buddy. He realized long ago that he wasn't the brightest bulb in town, but it didn't take a genius to know what you wanted to do with your life, and Buddy wanted to shoot bad people.

He considered himself the law in these parts, meaning this particular portion of Dalton County, Alabama. It wasn't a town or city that he patrolled, it was more of an area in between municipalities that went by the name of Hope Springs. He kept one hand on his sidearm and rubbed his pecker with the other. Buddy had kept a hard-on ever since he got in the woods, and now he really wished Lucille had come with him.

He entered the forest just after dark and his wristwatch now said it was three in the morning. The clearing must have been ten miles deep in the woods, and Buddy hadn't gone a night without making love to Lucille in almost a year. But he didn't take her to work with him since it was just too dangerous for a sweet little thing like her.

Buddy rubbed his pecker again and got distracted. He didn't seem to notice when the tendril of light crept toward the kneeling man and slipped into one ear, out the other, and then back in that ear to stay for good. The man named Terrence Wright always had a slim face with sharp features, but as his skin began to shine and his chin and ears stretched unnaturally, his features became more sinister than handsome. Terrence's eyes glimmered with the yellow of the tendril in his skull and he looked confused coming out of that trance for the first time. As his eyes dulled and regained a semblance of humanity once again, the hideous man turned from the blazing tree trunk and stumbled into the woods.

"Shit!" Buddy whispered. "Where did Mr. Wright run off to this time?"

Buddy adjusted himself one last time and rushed across the clearing, running past the magical lights and into the woods after the alleged molester. He kept his distance through the dark forest. He tracked the man mostly by the loud footsteps and grunting noises erupting from the brush ahead. Buddy had been hunting in those woods since he was a boy, and tracking a confused man through them at night wasn't all that difficult.

After hiking for over an hour, Buddy followed him out of the deep brush and onto the shore of a lake. At the edge, he squatted down and could barely make out what looked like a small pontoon boat on the water with Terrence inside. There was something snaking back and forth behind it.

But boats don't have tails, do they?

He saw two yellow dots staring back at him from inside the little boat, and in the moonlight he could make out a long-legged scaly thing floating in the water behind it. He only caught a glimpse before the floating creature and Mr. Wright turned the corner and disappeared around the bend.

That was a queer color for eyeballs to be, but Buddy didn't care about the molester's eyes. He just wanted to shoot the pervert.

As he walked around the lake to get back on the road, Buddy tripped and fell over a shadowy form at the water's edge. He stood up quickly and looked down to see a white-haired man in a lab coat curled up in a ball, sleeping soundlessly on the rocky ground.

Buddy shook his head at the sleeper. The sun would be coming up in an hour or two, so he decided to just leave the poor guy alone. He looked up at the stars shining over the lake. His eye was drawn to the shiny red dot that he believed to be Mars. He wondered what Martians were really like, and if he would ever get to see one. The red planet was especially bright that evening, and Buddy secretly wished Lucille could see it too.

Chapter 2

Hope Springs High School was nestled at the very edge of the woods. Outside of the two-story building that held students and teachers were several sports facilities and two parking lots, all of which were enclosed by dense forest. There was one road in and one road out, both of which wound through the mass of trees that gave the quaint little school that rural character parents were so proud of.

Katrina had spent most of the last seven years inside those trees, being taught things she wasn't sure she'd ever use again. Kat was a tall, skinny girl in her last year at Hope Springs. Senior year meant prom, graduation, and the general saying of goodbyes to pretty much everyone she knew. Although there were eighty-five other kids graduating with her, Kat didn't have one really close friend at that school she was going to miss. She didn't hate the other kids or anything, but that didn't mean she was going to miss them.

"In your precious name, I pray, Amen," said a prim and proper girl with legs neatly crossed.

Katrina looked up at the four praying teenagers in their school uniforms. They were seated in a circle of metal chairs at the front of an empty classroom at five o'clock on a Friday. She stopped going to church with her dad a year ago, but remained a member of the Hope Springs Student Christian Leadership Group. That meant staying after school every other Friday to watch the same kids talk about Bible verses and other things she really had no interest in anymore. The president of the group, Amy Plowman, had just finished her closing prayer, which she did at the end of every meeting.

"Now, everyone, remember to bring a friend next time," the group leader said.

"Why don't you bring your little brother, Kat? We brought Al," a girl named Julie said as the pimple-faced freshman next to her shamefully raised his gaze from Kat's tits.

"Trust me," she said as she stood up to leave, "he is not coming to a prayer meeting."

Katrina left the classroom carrying her laptop down the creaky hallway and out an exit door. The sun was so bright that it blinded her for a few seconds. She was standing on the sidewalk wincing, letting her eyes adjust, when she saw her little brother, Randall, get up off the grass and jog toward her.

He was in the seventh grade and had already changed out of his school uniform for the day. His t-shirt displayed a zombie Uncle Sam shooting the bird.

"How's the cult going?" he asked.

"They're not a cult," Kat said, her computer tightly clutched to her chest.

"That's your opinion," he said. "Why do you keep all those notebooks anyway? Why can't you just type things like a normal person?"

She strode off the sidewalk and into the parking lot. "I just like using a pen sometimes. They asked about you again. You sure you don't want to come?"

Randall giggled while walking to the passenger side of the little red sedan. "No thanks. You'll be the only Bible beater in college next year."

"There are lots of Christians in college."

"Yeah, right! You might spot a few unicorns, but if you really want to fit in, you'll hone your binge-drinking and blowjob skills this summer. They probably got a class for that kind of thing. The credits may not transfer, but at least you'll get into a sorority."

Kat glared across the top of the sedan.

"What's wrong with you?" she said, shaking her head. "You're thirteen years old. Shouldn't you be playing video games or something?"

"I don't like video games. You know that," he said as both of them got into the car. "I should have been born like a hundred years ago, back when kids weren't a bunch of over-stimulated dumbasses."

"If you lived back then, you would be climbing up chimneys or plowing a field for your pa," Kat said, starting the car. "You wouldn't be reading all day, that's for sure." She backed out of the parking space and drove out of the school parking lot.

"You should appreciate your older sister more," she said. "At least you don't have to ride the bus like the other kids your age."

"Yeah, I forgot how horrible that was. I mean, not one of those little creatures washed their hands. Disgusting."

He took a bottle of hand sanitizer out of a pocket and rubbed his palms with it. They rode down the long road that exited the school grounds, the car almost completely shaded by the trees on either side.

"I can't wait until you sound like Barry White and your face explodes with acne," Kat said.

"Who's Barry White?"

"I'm just glad it's the weekend," she said with a sigh.

That night, Katrina sat next to her brother at the table eating a home-cooked dinner. Her father was in his fifties, tall and skinny like Kat, and was the sweetest man she knew. Marla Thompson was around the same age, with an eighties-style perm and a deep Southern accent.

"You excited about the prom tomorrow?" Marla asked through a mouthful of meat loaf. "I never will forget mine. It was simply magical."

"I guess," Kat said. "I really don't want to go, and with Bobby of all people. He's a weird boy, Marla."

"Now, I don't know about that," her father said with a smile. "He always seemed pretty normal to me. I remember when he was a little boy running through the park with you and Daisy. The three of you used to be pretty close back then."

"When we were eight or nine," Kat said. "I've barely talked to him since we got to high school. I'm surprised he even asked me."

"Well, at least you're going," her mom said. "All young girls need to go to their prom. It's something you'll always remember."

"He's a good boy, Kat," her dad said, still smiling." You two should have a lot of fun."

She smiled back before catching Randall's grin across the table, making a circle with one hand and poking the index finger of his other through it over and over again.

"I hate you," Kat whispered.

"Stop that, son," her father said in as stern a voice as he could muster.

"Stop it, Randall," Marla said, slapping his hands down. "We all know she won't be doing any of that tomorrow night. Right, Kat?"

Katrina looked down at her plate and continued eating. It was quiet for a few moments, with only the sounds of chewing, silverware banging against plates, and the remnants of Randall's last giggle.

"You didn't answer your mother, Kat," her father said.

"Oh, right." Katrina sighed. "Of course not. We won't be doing any of that."

At least not with Bobby Funker.

Katrina shivered at the very thought and went back to eating.

"I wouldn't worry about her, Dad," Randall said. "That Funker's so stupid, he wouldn't even know where to stick it."

Marla almost choked with laughter, while her dad tried not to smile. He pointed toward Randall's room.

"Go on," her father said, grinning but trying to appear angry enough to teach the boy a lesson. "You're done eating anyway, and you're just being vulgar now."

"What did I say?" Randall asked.

"Go ahead, Randy," Marla said gently.

"Oh, alright," the boy said as he got up and stomped to his room.

After dinner, Marla went to the gas station to buy some cigarettes and check in on the new clerk working the night shift. She had been managing the Pumping Station for almost twenty years and liked to make surprise visits when a newbie worked alone for the first time. After she left, Kat and her father loaded the dishwasher together.

"You got any plans tonight?" her dad asked.

"Not really," she said, secretly knowing that he wanted her to run an errand. It was Friday night, and he always liked to send her on errands around the park on the weekend. "What's up?"

"Oh, nothing. I just needed you to go over and get the rent from Mrs. Jenkins. She leaves it in that little—"

"Yeah. Yeah," she said, leaving the dish-loading to her father and leaning against the counter. "She puts it in that little slot by the door, in an envelope that says RENT. I think I can figure that one out, Dad."

"Have you always been that sarcastic?" he asked.

"I'm sorry," she said, kissing her dad on the cheek. "Do you even know what sarcasm means?"

"Duh," he said. "I went to school too, you know."

Katrina left the trailer with her father's humongous key ring. It had Frank Thompson typed on it in bold letters. She walked along the gravel road that went through the center of the Belle Mobile Home Community. The sun was going down, and the moon was already showing in the daylight, something Kat always enjoyed watching. She waved at an older man seated on his porch to her left. He didn't wave back, but that was just Old Man Holmes. He never spoke to anyone.

To her right was a very large trailer, the largest in the park, with a sign in the front yard that said STODDARD FOR PRESIDENT. A very obese woman sat on the porch smoking a cigar in her nightgown. She glared at Kat as the girl hurried past the property line, trying not to look in the woman's direction. Everyone knew not to make eye contact with Ma Stoddard, not unless you wanted trouble.

A mean dog barked and she started jogging. The girl looked over her shoulder as she passed the next trailer to see the gigantic Mastiff named Bitch proudly seated at the property line, barking her head off at Kat. She jogged a little faster and turned around just as Bitch stopped barking. Kat grimaced as she remembered the bite-sized scar on her calf that the dog had given her years ago. She really hated that dog. She hated all the Stoddards, but she hated their dog most of all.

The girl walked to a stop sign and turned right, entering the front yard of a small, run-down trailer on the corner of Elm Street and Stoddard Drive. The wood creaked as she walked up the steps and approached the front door. The door had a weird-looking golden triangle hanging on it, but the porch was strangely empty. Mrs. Jenkins loved her plants and used to keep the front of her house full of them. Kat lifted the slot by the door and removed an envelope with RENT on the front.

The windows had curtains so she couldn't see inside, but outside the place looked vacant and empty. She stood on the porch, wondering if Mrs. Jenkins even lived there anymore. Kat shrugged and walked down the creaky steps back to the road, turning to look at the trailer one more time...and the blinds moved. She couldn't be sure if someone had moved it, but the blinds were swaying slightly back and forth like somebody had. As she squinted at that window, a booming voice startled her from a trailer across the street.

"What you see there, Kat?"

Katrina turned to see Beulah, a forty-something woman wearing a wide straw hat with a flowery bow wrapped around it. She was on her knees pulling weeds out of the small garden near her porch.

"You see anything interesting?" Beulah yelled.

"No, Miss Beulah," Katrina yelled, jogging over to the garden.

Kat bent down as Beulah tried to get off the ground.

"No need to get up, you just stay down there," Kat said, giving her a quick hug. "Where's Daisy?"

"She's out shooting that goddamned bow in the woods," Beulah said, still on her knees in the dirt. "I sure wish she could find a man. I tried to teach her how to cook and be feminine, but it never sunk in, I guess. I just don't know what I did to turn her queer. I love her either way, but..."

Kat bent down and gently touched her shoulder. "I'm sure it wasn't anything you did that made her the way she is, Miss Beulah. God just makes everybody a bit different, that's all. She's not gay either. You do know that, don't you?"

"Kat, you sure are a goddamned sweetheart," Beulah said. "Are you going to prom tomorrow night?"

"Yeah, I guess I'm going."

"You taking a boy with you?" Beulah asked, grunting and sitting up straight to face the girl.

"Bobby Funker."

"Shit," the woman said, shaking with laughter. "Little Bobby Funker. We used to call his daddy Mother Funker. Why are you taking him? You can do better than that little shit."

"He was the only one that asked," Katrina said.

Both of them turned suddenly at the sound of a trailer door slamming. They watched as a bald-headed twelve-year-old boy in a polo shirt and khakis walked off the creaky porch across the street and disappeared around the side of the mobile home. The boy didn't look their way at all, and his wrists, face, and hands were adorned with metal hoops, studs, and jewelry of all sorts.

"Well, it's a shame you couldn't get a proper young man to take you," Beulah said, still gazing across the street as the boy disappeared behind the mobile home. "I tell you what, that Jenkins boy really gives me the creeps. I think he killed her, you know."

"Killed who?" Kat asked.

"His momma," Beulah said. "Mrs. Jenkins. The queer thing is I haven't seen her in over a month now. She usually comes outside every goddamned day and tends to her plants, but they're all dead. I'm telling you, something's wrong in that trailer. The whole place just gives me the creeps. Back when Mr. Jenkins was around, they would come out and socialize sometimes, but he was a weirdo too."

"Wasn't he a teacher or something?" Kat asked.

"Sure was. Taught history back years ago. He quit when that devil boy was born. Seen some weird shit out of that family. Mr. Jenkins used to carry around some type of staff, as tall as he was. He would go off into those woods at all hours just like that boy does now. I'm telling you, the men in that family are full-on crazy. Just the other night, I saw that boy carrying a small coffin, not much larger than a three-year-old, into the woods."

"A coffin?" asked Kat. "Why didn't you tell my dad? He needs to know if stuff like that is going on in the park."

Beulah shrugged. "Well, I thought it was weird, but... I mean, my daddy had a coffin that he slept in for a while. He said it helped his sciatica or something. Anyway, the last month or so I've noticed his mom being gone, and that's what really worries me. Will you tell Mr. Thompson when you get home? Maybe he can go inside that place and check it out."

"I'll tell him," Kat said, "but she keeps paying the rent, so I don't think he can just break into her house like that. Maybe he can catch the boy and ask him."

"Already did that. I stopped him yesterday on his way into the woods and he just snorted and laughed. The weirdo didn't say a word."

"She's probably fine." Kat waved her hand and turned to leave. "Well, I'm gonna head back."

"Wait!" Beulah grunted and strained as she shifted on her knees. "Can you give this to Billy for me?"

She reached into her bra and pulled out a five-dollar bill.

"He went and got me drunk last night so here's his beer money," Beulah said. "Boy, that Billy sure can put it on good. I was sore as shit this morning."

Kat took the cash but avoided eye contact.

"Oh," the woman said. "I'm sorry about that, sweetie. Sometimes Beulah just gets carried away. You're old enough now where you should know about such things though. Do you know—"

"Yes," Kat said, putting her hand up and turning to walk away. "I know. Goodbye, Miss Beulah. I'll run the money by Billy's real quick."

"Bye, honey!" Beulah yelled at the fleeing teenager.

Chapter 3

Kat stood on a mat that read BILLY'S TRAILER and banged on the front door. She peeked in the window but didn't see anyone, so she walked around the side of the mobile home. She saw a young man about her age go inside the bright blue barn in the lot next to Billy's. Katrina took a deep breath and walked across the grass to the blue building.

She opened the tall barn door and stepped into a hallway with wooden pillars down the middle of it that ended in a large, open area. The barn looked much bigger on the inside.

To the left of her, Billy sat on the couch in front of a large TV. To her right was some kind of laboratory with beakers and vials everywhere. At the far end of the room was a closed door with a DO NOT ENTER sign on it.

Kat had never been inside the blue barn before. She took several tentative steps down the hall before stopping to watch Billy lean over the side of the couch and pull a can of beer out of the large cooler. Billy Miller was a middle-aged drunk who was proud of his mullet.

"Son! Bring Daddy some smokes on your way back in!" Billy yelled and clapped twice. "Hustle up, now!"

The teenager Kat had seen enter the barn was standing in the kitchen with a deadpan glare. She had known Cris for a year or so now, and it wasn't the first time she'd seen him glaring at his dad like that.

"Sure, Pop," Cris said sarcastically.

He was nineteen, tall, gawky, and very pale. He wore a buttoned-down shirt tucked into a pair of khaki pants. He walked around the couch and grabbed the pack of cigarettes off the coffee table that was directly in front of his father. Cris handed the pack to him and sat down on the couch next to his dad.

"Thanks," Billy said, staring lovingly at his son. "My seeed...my boooy," he slurred.

Kat watched as Billy lit a cigarette and took a long drag.

"You know that, right?" the man said through thick tobacco smoke. "I planted you in your momma's belly. You started from my seed."

Billy thrust his pelvis upward, cigarette dangling from his mouth.

"Real classy, Dad," Cris said.

Kat coughed to get their attention and stepped out from behind the hallway pillar.

"Stop it," Cris whispered, standing up quickly and peering toward the dimly lit hallway. "Someone's here."

"Is it that foul-mouthed heifer again?" Billy asked with eyes half-closed and pelvis be-stilled. "She better have my five dollars."

"It's not a heifer," Cris whispered just as Kat walked out of the hallway into the fluorescent lighting.

"Hey, Cris," she said, wincing at the alcohol smell. "Is that beer?"

"Beer...and farts, probably," Cris replied, trying not to make eye contact with the pretty girl. "How are you? Don't you have the prom coming up? Have you been here be—"

"Shit, boy," Billy interrupted, smiling at Katrina. "One question at a time will do. You got to pardon my seed, Kat. He's never been this close to a pretty girl before, at least not since he came out of his momma. How can I help you today?"

"I'm just here to give you this five dollars for Beulah," she said, handing Billy the money.

"Thank you kindly, ma'am," Billy said. "Would you like to stay for dinner? How about a beer?"

"She doesn't want a drink, Dad," Cris said. "She's in high school."

"I'll have a beer." Katrina shrugged. "Why not?"

Billy grinned from ear to ear as he reached in the cooler and handed her a beer.

"Why the hell not?" Billy said, still giggling. "I didn't know you drank."

"I don't," she said, popping open the can and sitting down in the only other piece of furniture on that side, a recliner at one end of the coffee table. She took a big gulp of the cheap beer and made a face.

"I'll have one too, I guess," Cris said, sitting down on the couch and taking a can from his dad. "So, is that all you came here for? To give him the heifer money?"

She was too busy looking around to reply. Kat had only peeked inside the open door once or twice before while running errands. Billy and his brother just finished building it a year or two ago, and they usually kept the door locked.

Katrina looked at the laboratory across the hall. There was a medical bed with a gurney on one side and built-in shelves from one wall to the next overflowing with old, dusty books. The floor was littered with even more books, stacked up six feet tall and side-to-side on two black rugs. There was a desk covered with glass containers and beakers filled with red, green, and other colored liquids. A green curtain walled off one side of the lab, and she could hear, for the first time, faint orchestral music coming from behind it. Kat downed half her beer and turned halfway around in her seat, still staring at the curtained-off area as she did.

Cris leaned forward nervously and asked, "Do you like classical music?"

"A little," Kat said, turning to smile at him.

Cris smiled back. "That's—"

"Mozart," Katrina interrupted. "It's a piano concerto."

"Wow." Cris took a sip of beer and got a little excited. "You do know your music."

"Not really," she said, putting the can down on the coffee table. "My little brother loves that stuff. I just know it from him. Personally, I prefer old jazz music. Stuff like Coltrane and Dexter Gordon. I have a bunch of jazz records at my house. What's wrong?"

Cris stared at her with his jaw wide open.

"He loves jazz," Billy said. "Be gentle with him. Be gentle with ma' seed."

A fly buzzed around Cris's head and landed on his lip, causing him to snap it shut and spit out insect germs.

"Stop saying that!" Cris said between spits. "Stop calling me your seed! It's disgusting."

"It is a little gross, Mr. Miller," said Kat.

Billy finished the beer and dumped his cigarette into the can before responding. "My apologies. Just not used to having a lady in the barn, I guess."

Suddenly, Katrina heard a commotion behind her and turned in the chair to see a wild-eyed man in a white lab coat throw the green curtain aside and stomp toward them. She had heard about Cris's uncle, but had never been this close to him before. The man looked older than Billy, in his fifties probably, with hair as white as his coat and oversized fish-eyes. He was holding a small axe in one hand. His bare feet were wrapped in plastic and the axe dripped green goo onto the wooden floor. The huge-eyed man stopped abruptly a few feet away from Kat.

"Professor, this is Katrina," Cris said nervously, leaning up in his seat and pointing to the girl. "She just came in to give Billy some beer money Beulah owed him, that's all."

Billy waved his hand toward the wild-looking man before speaking with eyes half-shut. "His name's Albert."

The Professor took a step closer to Kat. He bent down and studied her face for about two seconds, before standing upright and extending the non-axe wielding hand.

"My lady," the Professor said in an exaggerated British accent as Kat shook his hand. "It's a pleasure to meet you. Are you staying for dinner?"

"No," Cris said. "She has to get home tonight. Don't you, Kat?"

Kat saw Cris's nervous glance and thought he might be trying to warn her about something, but his face always looked nervous, so she really wasn't sure.

"Yes," Kat said politely. "I have to be leaving soon. I've eaten dinner already, anyway."

"Too bad," the Professor said, scratching his head and turning his back to them as he spoke. "I've got a possum boiling in the back. Killed it last night."

Kat looked over at Cris, unsure what to say about that.

"I think I'll eat at the house tonight. Alright, Dad?" Cris asked.

Billy snored on the recliner with an unopened can of beer between his legs.

"Yeah," Cris continued, getting up to leave and motioning for Kat to do the same. "I think I'm going home. You coming?"

Yeah," Kat said, standing up. "Sorry, Professor."

"Suit yourself," the man in the white coat said before rushing across the barn to the laboratory and leaning the axe against the desk. He began picking up the beakers and examining them one by one.

Kat started toward the door when she saw an open notebook on the coffee table and picked it up. There were lots of marked-through sentences and phrases but written in sloppy cursive writing in the center of the paper was PARANORMAL INVESTIGATIONS: CALL US IN YOUR TIME OF PERIL!

"What's this?" asked Kat.

The Professor rushed over, snatching the notebook from her and reading it slowly out loud.

"Paranormal Investigations. Call us in your time of peril," he said without the British accent. He stared wildly at the page, wheels turning furiously in his head.

Cris blew out a breath and started to say something but was interrupted.

"Looks like Billy's trying to come up with a name for our corporation. He has been trying to come up with a good one for…" the Professor trailed off, deep in thought before continuing with emphasis again. "How long has it been now?"

"Over five years," Cris said. "It's been five years that you two have talked about creating that thing."

"Five years," the Professor whispered while staring blankly at the far wall of the barn. "I saw those two young fellas on the TV the other day, the Ghost Chasers or something. That could've been us, me and Billy, it really could have. Five years. Has it really been that long?"

Cris snatched the pad from his uncle's hand and tossed it on the coffee table. The man didn't move a muscle, continuing to silently stare at the far wall.

"Yes, it has," Cris said, leading Kat away from the man in the lab coat. "Kat, let's go. I know you're in a hurry. Bye, Dad."

Billy snored louder. Kat saw him lazily lift his hand as if he heard the boy, and then she followed Cris out of the barn.

"So, let me get this straight," Katrina started as they closed the barn door behind them. "Your dad and uncle started a ghostbusters company?"

"Yeah, my dad's really into that stuff," he said as they walked across the grass to Billy's porch. "And the Professor—or Albert, as Dad calls him—got a degree in occult studies. Did you know he was a teacher at the university before my mom died?"

Katrina shook her head as they stopped in front of the porch and leaned against the rail. "No, I've never met him before today."

"Really?" Cris said. "Well, he's got like eight or nine degrees. We used to call him the Professor when he actually was one and it just kind of stuck. He was my mom's brother. Billy's just his brother-in-law, but when she died, both of them went a little cuckoo, and over the years they just got more and more cuckoo together. One day he quit his job at the college and my dad quit his job as a cop. They started talking about starting that business together shortly after that."

"I didn't know your dad was a cop," Katrina said. "Did they ever get any clients?"

"They got one. I think it was a missing dog or something. Woman thought it was Bigfoot that took it, but Dad was too drunk and the Professor was still too drugged up back then to find anything. That's when he started developing distinct personalities. I don't think they ever found that dog, and the woman came back and got her twenty-dollar refund."

"You mean he has multiple personalities?"

"Oh, he's got tons of them," Cris said. "It's usually different scientists or historical figures. Most of them lately have been from the nineteenth century for some reason. You don't really know which personality he is unless he signs his name or if the historical figure is someone you can easily recognize from the voice. Although, when he is Abraham Lincoln you just know, because he usually puts on one of those large hats."

"That is awesome," Kat said. "Who was he today?"

"Well, me and Dad have started tricking him into signing stuff every other day to find out. Usually, we get him to sign a check that we'll throw away afterward. The other day he signed as Baron Ludwig von Reichenbach, and from what we could find out that was a famous German chemist. So I guess that's who he is this week, but you can never really know with him."

"So, is your dad an occult expert too?"

Cris nodded. "It's the only thing I know of that Dad's an expert in. His alcohol-soaked brain may not retain much, but somewhere in there is a vast encyclopedia of weird stuff. He's been studying it all his life, and just about everything that's gone wrong in the world he thinks is related to something supernatural. Dad's kind of a conspiracy nut. You know, alien abductions, Kennedy assassination conspiracies, 9/11 didn't happen, stuff like that. What is it?"

Kat grinned from ear to ear. "Oh, nothing. I just got a wonderful idea. By the way, what should I call your uncle? Professor or Albert?"

"Just call him the Professor, but hopefully you won't have to talk to him again. He never leaves that barn. The man is very unstable. What's your idea?"

"I gotta go." She started walking away. "Talk to you later, Cris."

"Goodbye," he yelled, waving at her with both arms. "You can come over whenever you want. Don't be a stranger!"

Kat waved at him from the road and disappeared around the corner.

"Don't be a stranger?" Cris mumbled under his breath and lowered his hands. "Really cool, Cris."

Chapter 4

A SLOW, SAPPY LOVE song blared over the darkened dance floor. Katrina was swaying back and forth with a short, awkwardly skinny boy in glasses. The boy kept pushing the nosepiece with his finger so the glasses wouldn't slip off his nose.

"Ow!" Kat exclaimed as Bobby Funker stepped on her feet and said he was sorry for the sixth or seventh time that night.

Kat recovered and swayed back and forth again in a tight blue dress with her date's tiny hands on her hips.

"Ouch," she exclaimed, stepping away from the boy and kneeling down to rub her foot.

"Sorry," the boy said.

The slow music faded out, replaced with an edited version of a dirty rap song. The dance floor filled with teenagers. Katrina rushed past the empty tables and into the lobby. She stopped at the doorway and looked back to see Bobby doing the robot by himself, pausing to mechanically push up his glasses with one finger.

"If you leave, then you have to sign out," said the ancient woman from behind a desk. "Remember, you can't come back once you leave."

Katrina signed her name and stomped out of her Senior Prom without saying goodbye to anyone. She took a detour on the way home, turning down a dirt road about a mile before the trailer park and parking at a dead end. She walked barefoot, carrying her shoes down a tiny trail to the edge of Lake Warren. The sky was clear, and the full moon reflected on the top of the still, dark waters.

Lake Warren was a large body of water that flowed through several towns. It was where a lot of the locals who could afford boats went to sit on them and drink beer. Kat liked this particular shoreline since she could usually see a long way in both directions.

Katrina sat in one of the lawn chairs that her and Daisy had carried there a few weeks ago and watched the two full moons. She pulled the bottom of her blue dress off the ground and tucked it under her butt to keep it from getting muddy. She was graduating in about a month and still didn't know what she wanted to do with her life. Gazing down at the moon's watery reflection, the girl contemplated her options.

There was college, which probably meant junior college for her.

Work, which meant being a cashier at the gas station with her mom.

She could always find a man, have a baby, and be a stay at home mom, but just the thought of that made her laugh out loud. Her laughter was interrupted by a soft trilling sound, followed by a loud splash in the water.

She squinted and could just make out huge ripples at the center of the lake. It got very quiet for a few moments, and Kat felt eyes boring into the back of her head. The night suddenly felt ominous, and the mirrored moon looked more like a bony kneecap than the reflection of another world. Suddenly, she heard a cough...a human cough, and she tensed her entire body forward in the lawn chair.

"Hello?" said a human voice from behind her. "Is that a girl?"

She turned to see a skinny shadow with long gangly arms that almost made her scream with fright, until it moved closer and turned out to just be Cris.

"It's Kat," she said. "What are you doing here?"

Cris sat in the lawn chair farthest from her and said, "I should be asking you the same question. Pretty girl like you, out here all by yourself in a prom dress. What happened to your date?"

"Last I saw, he was doing the robot."

"You're kidding," Cris said with a deadpan gaze. "Did he graduate in the eighties?"

Kat giggled. "Since when did you get so funny? I thought you got nervous around girls."

"Only girls I can see," he said, squinting at her in the darkness, "and I can barely make you out."

She was smiling now and had forgotten all about weighing her future. "Do you come out here too?"

"Yeah," Cris said. "I got a lawn chair over there. I like to walk down here to get away from Billy and Beulah. They can get pretty loud on Saturday nights."

"Ew." Kat winced. "Please don't say that again."

"No! I didn't mean their sex sounds or anything. What I mean is that they sit on the porch and blare loud music. They sing along too. I usually just put on some headphones, but I like to get out of my room sometimes."

"Oh," Kat said. "What kind of music do they blare?"

"Elvis Presley. Some Dolly Parton. Beulah seems to have a thing for their gospel albums."

Kat suddenly realized she was having a good time. She reached across the empty lawn chair and grabbed Cris's hand. He looked away and squeezed it back.

"I'm glad you came out here. I feel a lot better now," Kat said.

"Anytime," Cris said, holding her hand as both of them gazed out over the water at the floating moon.

They sat for half an hour or so, making small talk in between the silence, then they headed back up the trail together. They got into Kat's car and were heading down the dirt road when she saw a man standing on the side up ahead and hit the brakes.

"Who is that?" Kat asked.

The man was dressed all in white and walking with his hands extended out in front of him. He was drunkenly swaying back and forth across the dirt road.

Cris let out a frustrated sigh and opened the door. "It's just my crazy uncle, sleepwalking again."

They helped the Professor into the backseat, drove the mumbling man to Billy's, and helped him out of the car.

"I'll take him to bed," Cris said, leading the man by the arm. "Just stay here, please."

"Alright," Katrina said as she watched Cris walk his uncle into the blue barn. In about two minutes, he returned with two beer cans.

"Is he alright?" Kat asked, taking a beer.

"He's fine," Cris said. "He's been doing that a lot as the German doctor."

"Dr. Reichenbach?" asked Kat.

"Yeah," he replied.

"So, does he just hear the voices in his head while he's the doctor?" asked Kat.

"He always hears voices in his head. Except when he was taking his pills, but he stopped filling that prescription years ago. The voices are just in German when he's that doctor."

"Huh," Kat grunted, imagining what it must be like to hear a tiny German homunculus yelling from somewhere deep inside her brain...something she quickly regretted.

"Personally, I think it's the voices that lead to the personalities," Cris said. "Either way, I figure his brain has got to be a crazy place to exist. I really feel sorry for him sometimes, but there isn't much we can do if he doesn't take his pills."

"Do they work?"

"They make the personalities stop. I believe they make the voices stop too, but when he takes them he just lies in the bed or sits and stares at the TV like a zombie. So, we don't push the meds anymore. We just try to keep an eye on him as best we can, but sometimes he still gets away."

"Cris," Kat said, guzzling her beer. "You have got to have the craziest family I've ever seen. No offense or anything, but between him and Billy you certainly have your hands full."

"Tell me about it," Cris said, taking a drink. "Well, I guess Beulah left early tonight. They're not on the porch and I don't hear them inside."

"Couldn't they be inside, you know, doing it?" Kat asked. The mental image of a naked Beulah and Billy tried to sneak in her brain and she fought it away.

"No. They gotta get good and wasted before they do that. Usually after midnight sometime." Cris looked at his watch. "It's not even eleven yet."

"Well, I need to get home, I guess. Eleven is my curfew tonight."

"You had a curfew?"

"Yeah," Kat said. "I could probably break it, but I'm actually kind of tired."

"Yeah, me too." Cris crossed his arms and shuffled awkwardly from foot to foot.

Maybe it was the moon, or the goofy way Cris held his beer and avoided eye contact. Kat didn't know why, but she suddenly felt the urge to kiss him.

She gently touched his cheeks and pressed her lips against his. It took a few seconds for him to kiss her back, but he did. It wasn't magical or anything, and Cris kept his eyes open the entire time, but at least she got a kiss on prom night.

Part Two: The Priest of the Dark Pit

Chapter 5

The Pumping Station was the only place to get gas in Hope Springs. It was also the only place to buy liquor, and although the grocery store next door sold cigarettes, the Pumping Station was much cheaper. Buddy was wearing a sleeveless white t-shirt tucked over his belly into a pair of tight white Wranglers. He wore an official-looking baseball cap with the word SECURITY on it. A holstered Glock dangled from his hip as he walked up to the counter and eavesdropped on Marla Thompson's cell phone conversation.

"Yeah, alright. I've got to go, Kat," Marla said, holding up a finger for Buddy to wait. "Love you too, honey."

He flashed a dangerous grin at Marla's tits as she hung up and let out a distracting cough.

"Up here, Buddy," she said, snapping her fingers to disrupt his booby trance. "You want some menthols?"

Buddy looked up and leaned forward on the counter, talking in his sexiest voice. "Hey there, hot stuff."

"Hey there to you too," Marla responded. "You done staring at my tits now? You ready for them menthols?"

"Sure,' he said, still looking her up and down. "Give me two packs today."

Buddy winked at her.

Marla rolled her eyes and turned around to grab the smokes as the man continued to explore her from behind.

"Yeah," he said, blowing out a heavy breath and standing up straight. He looked around the empty shop, having had his fill of Marla. "Lucille's got me smoking double-time lately."

She slapped the packs on the counter and spoke in a tired voice. "Anything else, Buddy?'

He slithered into sexy mode and whispered, "Yeah, how about bending down and getting me a box of rubbers, sweetie pie?"

The bell rang and he turned to see Terrence Wright enter with his eight-year-old daughter. Buddy quickly turned back around, closed his eyes, and decided he would just act like it was no big deal that the man he had been itching to shoot for over a month was in line behind him. His hand crept over his holster and Buddy took a deep breath. He opened his eyes to see Marla with her arms crossed. She pointed to the rack of condoms.

"They're right there, dumbass," she said. "I ain't got to bend down. There are six different kinds. Which one—"

"All of them," Buddy said nervously, his hand slowly sliding off the gun butt. "One of each."

"Alright," Marla said, grabbing six different types of condoms and shaking her head. "Lucille, Lucille. Poor little thing."

She rang up the cigarettes and condoms as Buddy leaned over the counter, swaying his backside with the VPL showing blue underwear through the white jeans. Terrence's daughter pointed and giggled.

Marla finished scanning the items and said, "That'll be thirty-seven sixty-eight."

Buddy straightened his back, rubbed his belly, and whistled. "Whew. That's kind of pricey for some rubbers. No worries though. I got the Benjamins."

He pulled a wad of twenties out of his front pocket and flipped two of them out.

"Give me those twenties," Marla said, snapping them out of his hand and getting the change. "You're holding up the line with all that stupid flirting. I am married, and you do know those ain't Benjamins, don't you?"

"What?" Buddy asked, putting the rest of the money away.

"Never mind. Here's your change. Now get out of the way."

Buddy grabbed his bag and tipped his hat to Marla before turning and walking past his nemesis. He slipped over to the candy bar section with his head lowered, occasionally glancing up to spy on the man and his daughter.

"Sorry about that. How you doing, Dolly?" Marla asked the little girl.

"Fine," the girl snapped back. "Why's that man wearing blue panties?"

"Well, you're quite an observant little girl, aren't you?" Marla said with a smile, looking to the girl's father now. "Can I help you, Mr. Wright?"

"Twenty dollars on pump three," Terrence said with yellow eyes and a goblin grin. "Can you break a real Benjamin?"

He handed her a hundred-dollar bill.

"Sure thing," Marla said. "Hold on a minute."

She went into the back room and Dolly examined a pile of business cards on the counter. The little girl took one while her daddy wasn't looking. The card said THE PARANORMAL AND NORMAL INVESTIGATORS on the top, and below that it said UNSOLVED MYSTERIES? CALL US TODAY! (888) MISTERY. There was also a cartoon drawing of a smiling ghost in the right-hand corner of the card. The girl giggled and quickly put the card in her pants pocket before her dad could catch her, just seconds before Marla came back to the counter.

"How's Mike doing?" she asked, handing the man his change. "Haven't seen him come in with you in a while."

The man turned his grinning face around without saying a word and led his daughter outside. Marla shrugged as Buddy crept back over.

"Terrence sure has been rude lately," she said, eyeing the door suspiciously for a moment before turning her gaze to Buddy. "What are you still doing here? Don't you have someone else to molest with those eyes?"

"Hey," Buddy said, pointing a finger at her and gritting his teeth. "I ain't no molester."

Marla grunted and began stocking the shelves while Buddy stood at the counter with his bag.

"Why don't you go on home to Lucille?" she said with her back turned. "I'm sure she's missing you pretty bad by now."

Buddy remembered his lover and adjusted his pecker. "It is quitting time, I guess. You be careful getting home tonight, Marla," he said, waving goodbye and briskly walking out of the store.

He walked across the parking lot and got into his beat-up pickup truck with the word SECURITY on the top of the windshield. Just as he started the engine and threw his elbow out the window, someone honked at him from behind.

"Hold up there," said an old man hopping out of the truck and approaching Buddy's window. "How's the patrol going?"

The old man was tall, with a bushy mustache and a SECURITY hat just like Buddy's. The holster on his hip was empty.

"Hey, Ralph," Buddy said through his open window. "It's pretty slow. I was just heading home to see the old lady, thinking about quitting for the day."

"Well, it's almost dark," said Ralph, turning back around. "I won't hold you up then. Hope you can make the meeting tomorrow night."

"What meeting?"

Ralph stopped and spoke from a few steps away. "We're gonna raid that pedophile camp. The little Pratchett boy went missing the other night. That makes ten of them."

"Ten in the last month?"

"Yup," Ralph said. "Be over at the preacher's place around six."

Buddy was excited. "I'll be there. See you, Ralph!" he said, waving out the window and driving off.

He pulled out of the gas station and traveled the half-mile to his trailer, which sat to the side of Highway 41. It had been a long day of patrolling the community. He and Ralph were the only members of the local security team. They swore an oath to vigilantly keep watch over the Hope Springs community and were known to make a citizen's arrest now and then. The county cops hated them, but if they were doing their job then there wouldn't be ten kids missing, and there wouldn't be the need for him and Ralph in the first place.

Buddy entered his trailer and threw the sidearm on the recliner. He rubbed his eyes and yawned before getting completely naked and jogging his jiggling, grinning self into the bedroom.

"I sure missed you, Lucille," he whispered, sliding under the covers and grinding his pecker against the silicone skin of his lover. He wrapped his arms around the life-sized inflatable sex toy and kissed the dark hole of a gaping mouth.

Chapter 6

THE PROFESSOR WRAPPED ALUMINUM foil over the stringy gray hairs on his scalp. He ran out of foil and looked in a handheld mirror to see that his entire dome was pretty much covered.

The voices in his head were nothing new to him. He had been ignoring them for most of his life. But there was something about the slithery, seductive speech that erupted in his brain a few hours earlier that frightened him. He didn't know exactly what it was yet, but it had scared him enough to wrap his head in aluminum foil.

The barn door flung open and Billy rushed down the hallway. He paused to stare at his brother-in-law with the shiny head for only a second or two before shrugging his shoulders and holding up a ten-dollar bill.

"You see this?" Billy asked.

The Professor stepped out from behind the desk and walked to within a few feet of Billy. He craned his neck forward and glared at the currency before whispering in an unsure voice, "Is it Monopoly money?"

"No," Billy said, snapping the bill proudly. "It's the real thing. Not only that, but you'll never guess who she gave it to."

"Me? No! You?"

"The Paranormal and Normal Investigators," Billy said. "We've got a paying customer."

The Professor's eyes bulged as he ripped off the foil and pulled at the tiny hairs on his head. He paced in a circle as he spoke. "How did this happen? We haven't advertised in years?"

"Beulah said we got business cards all over the place. There's some at the Pumping Station and there's even a website with a logo and everything."

"Someone's playing a joke on us," the Professor said, still pacing. "We haven't even set up the corporation yet."

"Beulah said it was Kat, that she's been promoting us for some reason," Billy said, putting the cash in his pocket. "I don't know why she done it, but it don't really matter. The point is, we got hired to do a job, and we need to make sure we don't mess it up this time."

"You're right. Who's the client?"

"Beulah," Billy said. "She wants us to find that nasty little dog of hers. Dirt Dobber. Should be easy finding an old dog."

"An old dog," the Professor whispered, nodding his head and rubbing his chin. He thought hard before snapping his fingers. "I got it!"

"You got what?"

"I know where that dirty dog is. I remember you telling me how Dirt Dobber got his name."

"He digs holes in her flower bed and tries to cover the dirt back over himself," Billy said, making pawing motions with his hand to imitate the little dog. "Kind of digs his own hole and buries himself in it."

"Yes! Don't you see?"

"No," Billy said, scratching his head and looking at his empty hand. "We got any beer?"

"Don't get drunk yet, Billy. Let's solve this case first."

"Right." Billy nodded with conviction. "So what were you saying?"

"Dirt Dobber is most likely in the dirt. The dog has dug a hole and buried himself in it," the Professor said, giggling like a madman and being fidgety. "He's probably having the time of his life, just wiggling around in that doggy grave of his."

Billy sighed at his brother-in-law, eyeing him suspiciously. "You drunk, Albert?"

"No."

"Have you been taking your medicine?"

"Uma-hun," said the Professor, digging into his lab coat and producing an empty baggy. "I took the whole thing this morning."

Billy's jaw dropped. "You smoked the whole bag?"

"What?" asked the Professor, leaning an ear forward. "What did you say?"

"You smoked the whole bag?" Billy asked louder, exhaling a breath and staring at the other man. "Albert, that was a lot of medicinal marijuana. It was supposed to last a couple weeks. Did it help with the arthritis?"

"Huh." The Professor considered the dilemma. "Well, first off, I didn't smoke it. I ate it. I read about pot brownies online and thought that seemed much healthier."

"Well, did it help?"

"Oh yes," the wild-eyed man said, doing a lunge then swinging his arms back and forth. "I have much more movement and the pain has been gone all day."

"Well, I'm surprised you're not watching cartoons," Billy said. "Anyway, so you're alright?"

"Never felt better."

"Good. It's just that if the little fella did, you know, dig a doggy grave and all, then he's probably dead by now," Billy said, still keeping a wary eye on his extremely stoned brother-in-law.

"Good. That'll make it that much easier to find him," Albert said, turning and walking back to his desk. He examined the spines of several thick books with one hand and waved the other at Billy. "Go on. Just look in your girlfriend's garden first. Then take a look at any pet cemeteries around here. Dig up the freshest grave you find."

"I'm gonna have a beer or three first," Billy said, walking to the cooler by the couch and extracting a can. He downed half of it before taking a seat on the cushion with a relaxing breath. "Then I'll go dig up some doggy graves."

"You better stop at three," the Professor said, wagging three fingers from across the barn.

Suddenly, a soft child's voice spoke inside Albert's head. It was gibberish, but somehow he knew what it meant. He looked over at Billy drinking his beer and decided it was safer not to tell him about the voice. The last time he had talked to his brother-in-law about them, he woke up in a hospital.

Billy called them multiple personalities, but the Professor knew that there were really only three of them. Over the years, he had murdered the other ones, and he was going to be taking out that German doctor any day now.

But people like the dear doctor didn't speak to him inside his head that clearly or anything, they just became him all of a sudden-like. The strange voices he heard that day were different. They were much more powerful than anything he had heard in the past, but it was probably just the brownies. The horrible voice of the creature he'd heard earlier in the day was gone for now, but this child's gibberish was still around, and it wasn't exactly comforting. He looked for the foil, but something in the gibberish told him it wouldn't work, so he just listened quietly. The child in his head wanted to meet him, and the Professor instinctively knew where.

"I'm going out," he said, feeling his body being pulled down the hallway and opening the barn door.

"Hey!" Billy yelled.

The obscenely high madman in the lab coat paused in the doorway and looked back at Billy.

"Can you check out Beulah's garden while you're out?" Billy asked.

"No time. You find the dog and I'll take care of the next client. Remember, only three beers if you're going to work today," the Professor yelled as he walked out of the barn.

"Three my ass," Billy said, downing the can and grabbing another one.

Albert Niederman walked to the back of the trailer park and into the dense forest. He couldn't hear the child's gibberish any longer, but still felt the presence of someone inside his head, silently directing him. It was sunset and the trail was getting darker. There was just enough sunlight for Albert to see up ahead where the trail seemed to end, but for some odd reason it never did.

He walked for an hour and the path still seemed to end in complete darkness at the same distance up ahead that it had when he entered the woods. It was a magical trail carved out just for him. When he looked behind him, the Professor could see where the trail began the way he had come, which didn't make any sense since he had been walking for over an hour. But neither did eating pot brownies and following a child's gibberish into the woods at night, so he just shrugged and kept moving.

It got even darker as he hiked deeper and deeper into the woods. After several hours, Albert couldn't see the head of the trail behind him anymore or much of anything in the blackness surrounding him. He kept walking anyway, trusting the magical path, knowing that if he zigzagged even a little then the path would still be there. Besides, he wasn't following the trail...the trail was following him.

He staggered through the darkness for hours. At last, he saw a light up ahead at the end of the magical path. As the tired man got closer, he was relieved to see that the trail didn't go on forever anymore. His legs ached and the arthritis in his hands and back burned. He really wished that he still had some medicine left.

"Professor."

It was a child's voice, but it took him a moment to realize that it wasn't inside his head. The voice was faint and coming from the light-filled cave up ahead. At the cave entrance, the shadow of a hand beckoned him inside. The weary man walked into the cave on wobbly knees with shoulders slumped.

Inside was a fire with a young, bald-headed boy sitting cross-legged on the ground behind it. It was the Jenkins boy and, as usual, he was adorned with bracelets on his wrists and ankles, rings on his fingers, metal jewelry looped through his eyebrows and fingernails, and large studs shone from his neck, nose, and mouth. He also wore several thick necklaces with objects dangling from them. Curiously, the boy seemed overdressed for a cave visit, wearing a short-sleeved polo shirt tucked into khaki pants. The boy's colorful tattoos wound around his forearms and neck, covering most of the exposed flesh there.

"Jenkins boy?" Professor timidly asked.

"Is that what they call me?" the boy replied.

The Professor nodded.

"I'm no longer a boy. Why don't you just call me Mr. Jenkins."

The Professor nodded again and wondered if it was possible to die from a brownie overdose. He shook the cobwebs out of his brain and responded. "Mr. Jenkins, why did you drag me here? I mean, I'm assuming that was your voice in my head today."

"It was. I apologize for interrupting your evening, but I am in need of another wizard. There is a spell I must cast and it calls for two natural-born, human wizards. I tried conjuring one up, but that didn't work since they weren't born right. Then I contacted the schools, but it was way too expensive to rent a wizard, since they're on the other side of the country and all. So, I had to improvise and... Voila! Here you are."

The Professor was still studying the cave as the child spoke to him. The rock walls were covered with strange writing and symbols, and he was just about to walk over and examine one of them when an understanding of what the boy just said somehow solidified in his gray matter.

"A wizard?" the Professor asked, turning his gaze across the fire to the boy. "Are you calling me a wizard?"

"Well, yes. That's what you are, isn't it?"

"No!" the Professor said emphatically. "I'm no wizard. I've never cast a spell or done any magic tricks."

The child giggled to himself and spoke in a gentle voice. "Just because you haven't practiced any wizardry doesn't mean you are not a wizard. You see, you are either born that way or you're not. Many people are born with the gifts of magic and never even know it. I know it might come as a bit of a shock, but if you heard my voice inside your head today, then you are a wizard."

The Professor walked to the side of the fire and sat on a big rock. He put his head in his hands and moaned, trying to process all that was going on. If he was hallucinating or dreaming, then he would come out of it eventually anyway. If he wasn't, then the boy was obviously crazy.

"Alright," the man began, avoiding eye contact with the creepy boy in khaki pants. "Let's say that I'm not hallucinating or dreaming. In that case, how do you know that I'm a wizard? You spoke to me, but you could have picked anyone, right?"

"No. That's precisely it. I spoke to every living thing within a few hundred miles in a language that only wizards can hear and understand. The fact that you understood and came here proves you are one."

"I see. And nobody else has come by tonight?"

"No, and they won't either. There were others that heard me, but they were so far away that I decided to release their minds. I chose you mostly because of your location."

"I guess it couldn't have been the massive amount of THC in my system?"

The boy shook his head. "No, the drugs can open you up to hear voices of various kinds. You know, ghosts, beings from other dimensions, and things like that. In enough doses, they can enhance any psychic abilities you may have for a bit. It might help with such parlor tricks. However, there are no drugs you can take that will allow you to hear the calling of a wizard if you are not one yourself. When the message goes out, it's like a dog whistle for our kind. Civilians are incapable of understanding it, no matter how drugged up they are."

"I see," the Professor said. "How did you learn all this stuff? I mean, you can't be over eleven years old."

"I just turned twelve."

"Happy birthday."

"Thanks," the boy said, taking a deep, relaxing breath before continuing. "Let's see, how did I learn about wizardry? Well, my mom of course. I was home-schooled by her."

"Mrs. Jenkins was a witch?"

"Yes, but not a very good one. She just dabbled in potions mainly. However, she sold enough of her creations to pay for a mentor for me. If not for her, I would have never got into the university. You see, there are two magical colleges in the United States, the one in San Diego and the other in Portland, Oregon. I start the Portland School of Magic and Sorcery next week," the boy said proudly.

"Why are all the schools out west?"

"Beats me," the boy said, taking another deep, relaxing breath. "That's one of the rules of wizardry though. You must accept the world for what it is. It roughly translates to just staying calm and dealing with whatever happens to you. That's why wizards are always so calm under stress."

The Professor glared his bug-eyes at the boy and his shoulder twitched nervously.

"At least that's what the textbooks say and all. You're kind of an exception to that, I guess," said the boy. "You seem like the nervous type. What did you do before you found out you were a wizard?"

"Let's see," the man said, pondering his life for a moment. "I have a Masters in Biology, Chemistry—"

"You're a scientist?"

"Kind of," the Professor replied. "I do have a lab at the barn."

"Splendid," said the boy. "You would probably enjoy making potions, and that doesn't really involve much spell casting, so the whole 'staying calm' thing may not necessarily apply to alchemists. Perhaps it's just major spell casting that the rules of wizardry are really meant for. What's wrong?"

The Professor held his head and spoke quietly. "I have a headache."

The boy snapped his fingers and the headache was gone.

"How did you do that?" asked the Professor.

"How do you think?" asked the grinning boy. "Magic. Anyway, if you would like to apply to one of the colleges, you'll need a letter of recommendation. I can give you one since you need at least two to get in."

"I have nine degrees. I think I'm done with school."

The boy took a deep breath, stretching his arms above his head in a yoga pose.

The Professor shrugged his shoulders before breaking the silence. "Well then, what do you want? Either this is a dream or it isn't, but either way, I'll play along. I guess I'm a wizard, so let's just get on with it."

"Oh wonderful," said the boy, clapping his hands together and smiling at his guest. "I like you already."

Suddenly, the clanking sound of steel and a monstrous grunting noise erupted from the mouth of the cave. The Professor turned his head to see a gigantic medieval knight approaching them dressed in black armor and holding a humongous battle-ax. The black knight stood over seven feet tall and wore a dark mesh of chain mail with arms and legs protected with thick, void-colored leather. In the little semicircular opening in the helmet where a face should be, there was only formless black leather with no eyes. The knight came to a stop a few feet away, breathing heavily through the dark cloth.

The newly minted wizard put his hands up and stepped back. Mr. Jenkins gently placed his palm on the shoulder of the lab coat.

"What is it?" asked the Professor, trying to stay calm.

"His name is Reginald and he won't hurt you," the boy said, glaring at the knight. "He is one of my children and would never hurt another wizard."

"Is that the creature that was in my head earlier today?"

Jenkins gave a startled look at the twitching man before responding. "You heard another voice today?"

The Professor nodded, trying not to look in the direction of the gigantic knight, who just stood there breathing heavily. "I thought it was a pretty big coincidence, hearing two different voices in the same day."

"There are no coincidences," the boy muttered to himself, before continuing in the normal tone again. "Was it a slimy, wretched voice?"

"Yes, and I tried putting foil on but it didn't work."

"Aluminum foil?"

"Yeah," said the Professor, cowering closer to the boy, "but it didn't work."

"Of course it didn't work," Jenkins said with a laugh. "It's just aluminum, you silly monkey. That entity that you heard is one of the reasons I need to do the spell. It's one of the reasons I brought you here. Believe me, it wasn't Reginald. The black knight would make a dangerous foe, but under my control he is no danger to you. Besides, he doesn't have any psychic ability whatsoever."

"How do you know?"

"Because I created him. He was conjured out of my own imagination," the boy said, tapping his skull. "I've been coming out here deep in the woods to practice my magic without anyone else around. There's a conjuring spell that I've been practicing for years, which basically allows me to create animate or inanimate objects, pretty much anything I want, out of my imagination."

"So you just mumbled some things and that knight magically appeared?"

"No," said the boy, casually reaching up and rubbing his hands above him. He plucked a glowing strand of light out of his bald head like it was a stringy hair. "It's more like pulling the images from my mind and letting them form on their own. Reginald began as a strand of light, just like this one, and so did all the other beings I've created over the years."

"There are others?"

"Oh, yes," the boy said, bringing the strand of light downward and gently blowing on it as it vanished completely. "I couldn't control a few of the early creations and they got loose of my strings. I've regained most of them and they'll soon be as bound to my mind as Reginald. However, I'm afraid that some things, like that dreaded, hooded creature, have become hopelessly independent and can't be tamed. Sometimes I wish Mother had never told me those awful bedtime stories."

"So you have creatures, other than Reginald here, that you control? There's a hooded creature you let loose from your imagination and it's out of control now?"

"Pretty much," the boy said.

"How many others are there?"

The boy shrugged. "I'm not really sure. I was not as disciplined when I first started, and sometimes they would get a mind of their own. There are certainly others, but this dark priest is especially wicked. It's already killed dozens of people, and I feel that it's my responsibility to stop it."

"Before you leave for school, you mean?"

"Yes," the boy said, "but there is still the matter of that slithery-voiced thing that spoke to you earlier today. I think that Maggie's brood may have conjured up something ancient."

"Who the hell is Maggie? Is she another wizard like you?"

"She's the first child I created. You see, all the creatures I conjure up are wizards too. I mean, I'm one, so it would seem foolish to create a bunch of non-wizards to hang out with. Why would I want to do that? It would be quite boring and we'd have nothing to talk about. Anyway, I almost have her back in control now, but while she was loose, I believe Maggie may have conjured up a whole community of creatures capable of summoning spells. I'm not really sure who summoned the thing or even what it is yet, but whatever the entity calls itself, that's what I think is speaking to you. I can hear its quite unpleasant voice sometimes too. Whether it was one of Maggie's kind that did it or not, there is definitely something loose out there that is trying to obtain a following for its Master. When something like that gathers enough people, it can actually become extremely dangerous. Since I created Maggie and just about every unnatural thing within a hundred miles or so, I'd really like to clean up my mess before whatever it is begins a calling of its own."

"Was that what I heard? This thing calling me to join some cult?"

"Yes, and its Master is powerful. I believe it lurks just outside our existence, waiting for someone to summon it, to bring it here into our world. I don't know who started the spell of bringing something like that here, but once it gets enough people to pay attention to its message, then a large following could drag its Master completely into our realm. I doubt it has good intentions, from what I've heard so far."

"It sounds kind of nasty," the Professor said.

The boy nodded. "It is. I had to get you here to begin a spell. Spells are not just poofs and smoke. They're much slower than that. They're like a kind of plan you put into motion...a chain of events, and to begin this one I had to have another wizard. I just can't leave things like they are. I'm sure that students get kicked out of school for that kind of stuff. You know, being responsible for resurrecting an ancient evil cult and all."

"I see your point," Albert said, clapping his hands together. "Well, it seems you need another wizard for this spell of yours. What do you need me to do?"

The boy grinned and stood up. He was under five feet tall, but suddenly the child loomed larger than the gigantic knight. The Professor's body tingled as the reality of the cave became distorted. The knight vanished, replaced with a rippling of space where it once stood.

The boy shrank back down to normal size and took a deep, relaxing breath before speaking. "This conversation is for our ears only. We can't have giant medieval knights out there knowing the future, now, can we?"

"No, I guess not. So, what do you need from me again?"

"Just a piece," the boy said, growing in size once again and glaring downward at the Professor with a grin full of teeth. "Just a little piece of you, and then I'll sew you right back up again. You won't feel a thing. For the rest of this life, you'll never even know it's gone."

Albert didn't feel much like a magician when he woke up in front of the barn the next morning. His whole body ached, except for his head, as he brushed the grass off his lab coat and entered the blue building to see Billy snoring on the couch in a pair of tighty-whities.

The Professor went into the barn bathroom and took a long, hot shower, trying unsuccessfully to scrub away the memories of the previous night. He walked naked across the barn and put on a fresh t-shirt tucked into a pair of scrubs and one of the ten or so clean white lab coats that hung in the closet in his bedroom. His bedroom consisted of an open area of the laboratory walled off by green curtains. His closet consisted of a wheeled clothes rack that stood next to a pair of mattresses stacked on the wooden floor.

After getting dressed, he threw back the curtains and saw a little girl standing in the hallway with long brown hair. She had her hands on her hips, which were cocked to one side in a cute, *I'm gonna tell you something now* stance.

"Howdy!" the girl exclaimed.

"Howdy," the Professor replied, giving the girl a military salute for no reason at all and then noticing it halfway through and clutching the side of his face in confusion. His eyes never left the girl. "How long have you been in the barn?"

"A while. I seen your thingy, you know," the girl said proudly. "I seen it dingle dangle when you was running."

"You did, huh?" he asked, unsure if that was the right response. "First one?"

"No. I got an idiot brother," the girl said, as if it was a stupid question. She pursed her lips and looked the man up and down.

The Professor considered a follow-up question, but decided against it. He really needed to change the subject from dingle dangles to something, anything else. "Nice morning, isn't it?" he asked, and looked up at the barn roof uncomfortably.

The girl finished her analysis of him and did not look impressed. "I seen you in the yard and was scared to come in at first. I thought you was a monster."

"No monster," the man said, his eyes drifting slowly from the ceiling back to the girl. "Just a wizard."

"A wizard?"

"Maybe," he replied, unsure if the dream from the night before had any truth to it or not. It didn't matter though. He would pretend it did for the moment. He kind of liked the thought of being a wizard.

"What kind of wizard are you?" the girl asked. "The Merlin kind, or more like Harry Potter?"

"Neither. I don't actually know any spells."

"Like Rince Wind then. He only knows one spell and people don't think he's a real wizard either."

"If he knows one spell, then I don't know if I'm like him or not. You see..." He trailed off, deciding to change the subject again. He was going nowhere with the magic talk. "They call me the Professor. What's your name, little girl?"

"I'm Dolly."

"Nice to meet you, Dolly. Now, what do you want?"

The girl took a business card out of her pocket and looked down at it as she spoke. "I didn't know if you could really help me or not. Do you handle paranormal and normal investigations?"

He eyed her suspiciously. "Maybe so."

"Is it just you and that snoring man on the couch?"

"Yup. You got a dog for us to find or something?"

He didn't really like children in the first place, but especially not unwanted children in his barn before he had his morning coffee.

"I ain't got a dog. I am missing a brother though. Since you're a wizard, have you got a crystal ball or anything? I'd like to locate him as soon as possible." She put the business card back in her pocket and pulled out a hundred-dollar bill. She handed it to the man. "Here. I figure this should work for a deposit, and if you can find him then there is plenty more where that came from. It's called a Benjamin."

The Professor took the bill and tried to act professional. "Where did you get this kind of money, little girl?"

"My daddy's wallet. He's got tons of them."

The man thought for a moment, stuffed the money in the pocket of his lab coat, and extended his hand to the girl. "You have a deal. Let me have my coffee and we'll get to investigating."

The two ironed out the particulars in the hallway before the Professor escorted her outside and closed the barn door. He walked to his desk and sat down, rubbing his arthritic knees. The bag of medicine lay empty on the floor. He tried to forget about the aching joints and remember more of the dream from the night before.

He remembered being told that he was a wizard and seeing that boy's menacing face hovering over him right before he woke up on the lawn. He could clearly remember the voices in his head, and figured he had probably fallen asleep somewhere in the woods and just dreamed everything in the cave. Oh, he also remembered something about a wizard college in Portland, of all places, and there was some mission or task to do...and he had a sense that he had lost something in the woods, but had no idea what it could be.

Chapter 7

Belle Trailer Park was located along a straightaway off Highway 41 and was the only mobile-home community in Hope Springs. All eighty lots were lined up in rows along streets of gravel that crisscrossed through the park. At the entrance was a large, tattered sign with BELLE on it. The entire place was bordered by a forest that blanketed everything and everyone in Hope Springs.

It was a Saturday in the middle of May when Katrina turned off the highway and into the park for what seemed like the millionth time. She was thinking about her graduation on Thursday, which was a purely symbolic event since she had already attended her last day of high school ever.

She parked the car in front of her home. The girl turned the knob and was surprised to find that it was locked. Kat banged on the door and her father opened it with a smile on his face.

"Since when do we lock the doors around here?" Katrina asked, giving her dad a kiss on the cheek and taking a seat at the kitchen table.

"Since that child molester got on the loose, that's when," her dad said, locking the door. "You haven't heard about the missing boy?"

"Yeah, I heard about him last month. But it's only one kid. Kids go missing all the time. I bet if it wasn't a white teenager from that mega-church then you wouldn't even have heard about it."

He leaned against the oven. "You're probably right about that first kid, but the other nine have been pretty diverse."

"Nine?"

"Yup," her father said. "There have been ten kids abducted in the last month. The most recent one was from this park. You know the Higgins girl?"

Kat nodded. "Kind of. I've seen her around a few times, but don't really know her. She's like eight or something."

"Well, Mr. and Mrs. Higgins are going crazy right now. I just came from their place. The cops were there and everything."

"It just happened?" asked Katrina.

"Been missing since yesterday," he said. "I'm telling you, it's one of those child molesters over at the preacher's place. You stay away from there, alright?"

"Don't worry about that," Kat said, grinning and moving toward the living room. "I never liked that preacher, even when he was at our church."

"Well, Brother Pruitt means well. It's just those molesters take advantage of him. Now, I was never for running them out of town when they first got here. Maybe I should have, but he's a sweet-natured man and is just trying to be Christ-like. I can't really blame him for that."

"Where's Mom?" Kat asked. "Shouldn't she be home by now on a Saturday?"

"She had to stay late. That new kid didn't show up again for his shift. She's gonna be a while."

"Teenagers are so unreliable these days," Kat began, shaking her head. "Minimum wage just isn't good enough for them, is it?"

"Hey, can I rely on you for something?" her dad said with a grin.

"I stepped right into that one, didn't I?"

"Kind of. I need you to go over and get the rent from Mrs. Jenkins. She leaves it in that little—"

"Yeah. Yeah," Katrina said, getting up and heading for the door. "She leaves it in the little slot by the door, in an envelope that says RENT. I think I can handle that one, Dad."

Kat walked out the door and started down the gravel road. She passed the Stoddard trailer without so much as a bark from Bitch and went around the corner to the Jenkins home. Across the street, Beulah wasn't home. The Jenkins trailer was silent and the sun was setting.

A chill crept up her spine as she stepped onto the porch and retrieved the envelope. She turned her back on the front door and felt a pair of eyes watching the back of her head, but she didn't dare to look. Katrina just kept on walking, around the corner and down the street to Billy's trailer.

As the girl walked across Billy's front yard, she saw the Jenkins boy carrying a small coffin into the woods at the end of the road. Something fell out of it that looked like a huge test tube filled with water, and the boy calmly picked it up and placed it back in the coffin. He saw Kat and flashed a smile so fake that it chilled her spine. She did not smile back as she watched him disappear into the trees.

"Kat!" Billy yelled from his porch. "What you looking at?"

"I'm not sure," she replied, jogging onto the porch to see Billy and Beulah in rocking chairs with an open cooler between them. "Where's Cris?"

"What you want with Cris?" Beulah asked, not really looking at Kat. She was drunk and had a confused look on her face. "Billy, are they doing it? Did you have that talk with Cris yet?"

"I had the talk," Billy said, before chugging his beer and burping loudly. "Now, Katrina, if you need any condoms, don't be afraid to ask me or Beulah. Understand?"

Kat rolled her eyes. "No thanks. Now, where is he?"

"Cris is helping Albert with something," Billy said, pointing to the barn where loud mechanical noises were erupting. "He'll be back in a minute. Want a beer?"

"No thanks," Kat said. She considered going to the barn, then changed her mind. There was no telling what they were doing in there.

"You hear about the Higgins girl?" Beulah asked, her eyes fully open now that she was gossiping.

"Yeah, I heard she went missing," Katrina replied, leaning against the rail.

"Yup, and there's been others too," Beulah said. "I'm telling you, it's that child molester camp behind the preacher's place. He's got four or five registered sex offenders living on church property out there. He's supposed to be trying to reform them or something. Pedophiles for Jesus, I guess."

"Listen." Billy lifted his can of beer. "You don't know that those men did anything. Everyone needs to let the police do their job and stay out of it."

"I just don't like it," Beulah continued. "Those nasty men that close to us. It's only a mile down the road. Poor Daisy goes that way through the woods to the archery range just about every day."

"I think Little Miss Rambo can take care of herself," Billy said. "And as for the molesters, they probably aren't bad people. A few of them may have even been wrongfully convicted or something. And what if they did mess with some kid? That doesn't necessarily make them evil or anything. They could have reformed, or just be really good people and molest kids sometimes."

"Billy!" Beulah exclaimed in horror. "If they're molesting kids then they can't be good people. I don't know how you can think that."

Suddenly, the barn doors flung open. Loud sawing noises erupted from within as Cris ran outside. He jogged across the yard on his tippy-toes, arms swinging daintily at his side.

"There he is," Kat said, smiling as she watched him stop at the porch steps.

"There's my boy," Billy said, pointing his beer at Cris. "Ma—"

"No, Dad," Cris said, pointing back at the beer. "You promised. No more calling me your seed. Remember?"

"Touche," Billy said with a nod. He lit a cigarette and changed the subject. "Well, what do you think, son? Does molesting a child make you a bad person?"

Cris didn't answer. He glared briefly at his father before escorting Kat into the house. She followed him through the living room with walls covered in images of UFOs, ghosts, and other paranormal phenomena. She had been in the place before, but the pictures that were pinned to the walls changed all the time.

"It's amazing that you actually got an education," Kat said as they walked into Cris's bedroom. "When did he take you out of Hope Springs?"

"Oh, about six years ago," Cris said, sitting down at the edge of the bed. "Yeah, it's amazing to think that the drunk on the porch was my math, science, and English teacher...and I'm not insane. I'm not insane, am I?"

"No," Katrina said, sitting next to him on the mattress. "You are perfectly normal. That's what is so confusing. So what were you doing with the Professor?"

"Just making stuff. I have no life, so I hang out with my crazy uncle in his barn laboratory for fun. He had his table saw out and was making something out of wood. I think it's another box. He keeps making these boxes to put over his head, to keep out the voices and everything."

They both giggled nervously. Kat walked over to the record collection and put on a John Coltrane album before sitting back down beside him. She played with her hair while Cris squirmed.

"So," Cris said, "you decided to start the junior college this summer, huh?"

"Probably. Are you going to school?"

"Yeah. I'm going there in the fall. I'll probably binge drink and party all summer. You know, to prepare for college."

"That's what my little brother keeps saying," Kat said. "I don't think everyone will be getting drunk and having sex in college. Do you?"

"Um, I don't know," Cris said. "Kat, we've been fooling around for the last month, but I was wondering if you ever thought about doing other stuff?"

"Like what?" Kat said with a grin. She liked to see Cris squirm.

"Oh, I don't know. Other stuff."

"You mean have sex?" Kat asked. "Is that what you mean?"

"Sure."

"Have you ever done it before?"

"Once. It was about a year ago and she's not around anymore or anything. Like most things in my life, it was quite a strange experience."

"What was it like?" Kat asked.

"You've never done it before?"

Kat shook her head.

Cris took her hand. "Listen. My first time was awful. Hopefully, yours will be much better."

"Who was it with?"

Cris sighed. "You see, Daisy has a cousin named Leslie, and this cousin was visiting one weekend. It was a Friday night and she was drinking on the porch with us. She's a couple years younger than me, but a real horny girl. I don't have a high tolerance for alcohol, so I got sick and was inside puking my guts out. When I looked up from the toilet, Leslie was in the bathroom with me and she had her shirt off. So, we got naked and she had me sit in the bathtub while she rode on top of me or whatever."

Cris grew quiet and stared absently at the wall. Kat elbowed him.

"Hey," she said. "Finish the story."

"Yeah, so anyway. She was on top of me and it was awkward and everything since I was floating in and out of consciousness, but right as we got started my stomach got real upset. So, I spewed chunks all over her breasts."

Kat laughed so loud she snorted.

"Please don't laugh," Cris said.

"I'm sorry. Did you at least get off first?"

"No. I never got around to that." Cris squirmed on the mattress. "Now you got to tell me your most embarrassing sexual escapade since I told you mine."

"But I'm a virgin. I don't really have any."

"You've done other stuff, haven't you?" Cris asked, squeezing her hand a little tighter. "Come on, that was a pretty big secret I told you."

"Oh, alright," Kat said, her cheeks turning red. "I went to my junior high dance with, oh, what was his name? Theodore... Theodore Bandy, that's it. He was kind of overweight and shorter than me. We were dancing to some fast song and I had on a dress and everything. He kept swinging his arms back and then forward again, and his arm kept going to one side of me then the other, like a long-armed ape or something. On the final swing of his arm, he had his fingers extended and curled like a fishhook. The hand swung right up under my dress, smacked my panties, and the curled finger hit its mark. He hit me hard enough to hurt. The boy looked like he'd just murdered someone. Then, for some odd reason, he sniffed the finger and ran off the dance floor. I was mortified and never told a soul until now."

"I will guard that secret with my life," Cris said. "I'm not sure whether that's technically first base or second, but it sure counts as something. So, he didn't apologize or anything?"

"Nope. He never mentioned it to anyone and neither did I."

"Those are two awful experiences," Cris said, looking into her eyes. "Maybe one day we'll have better sex stories to tell."

"God, I hope so," Kat said, looking away. "Oh, I almost forgot why I was here. Did your dad get any calls from all those business cards I sent out?"

"Yeah. They got two new clients. Beulah and some little girl."

"Great!" Kat said. "I want you to get your dad and the Professor to meet us in the barn tomorrow night. We need to have a meeting. It will be the first official meeting of the Investigators."

"You mean, you want to help them investigate or whatever?"

"Sure, don't you?" Kat asked.

"Why not? What else am I gonna do?"

"Great. Tomorrow night then," she said, getting up to leave.

"Sure, but don't you want to stay?" Cris asked, lowering his voice in an uncomfortable attempt at seduction.

Kat looked down at him, seated pitifully on the bed. He was trying to avoid her gaze after realizing the seduction hadn't worked. She sat back down.

"Cris, I'm just not ready to have sex yet. Maybe later on, but for now I'm just not ready. Is that alright?"

"Of course," Cris said. "I just didn't want you to dump me. I can wait as long as you want."

That was what she loved about him the most, his kindness. Kat kissed him and the two teenagers fell onto the bed together. As they held each other and kissed with eyes closed, neither one of them could see the glassy-eyed, scaly thing watching through the window. The huge, frowning fish face filled the frame that was almost ten feet above the ground outside. The jazz saxophone drowned out the purring, trilling noise of the greenish-colored creature as it stared lovingly at the couple on the bed.

Chapter 8

DAISY HAD TO WAIT ON BOY-TOY TO GET OUT OF CHURCH. WHERE U?

ON THE WAY!

GROOVY

Groovy?

Cris ended most of their conversations awkwardly, but she was used to it by now. Katrina smiled and put the phone in her pocket as she jogged through the park. It was Sunday night and her parents would have already dragged her brother to church by now.

She turned the corner and hurried toward the blue barn with no windows. There weren't any outside lights on, and in the blackness of night it looked dark and creepy. She stopped in the grass and considered where to hang some outside lights to keep from scaring off potential customers.

"Kat!"

She turned around to see a short, muscular, twenty-two-year-old girl in tight shorts with a holstered pistol around her waist. It was Daisy, and she jogged right up to her and gave Katrina a hug.

"Congratulations, honey!" Daisy said.

"Thanks."

Daisy's boyfriend came running up and stood next to her. Willard Camp was a Math teacher at Hope Springs. Kat never had his class. He was tall and looked like a Ken doll.

"How does it feel to be leaving that place for good?" Daisy asked.

"Feels great. I'm just ready for it all to be over with."

"Yeah," Will said, brushing a lock of blond hair from his eyes. "I remember that feeling."

"By the way," Daisy interrupted. "Beulah said you were at Billy's house kind of late last night. What were you doing over there?"

"I went to see Cris."

"You banging him yet?" Daisy asked.

"I'm not banging anybody. We're just friends," said Kat, turning toward the barn. "You coming?"

"Sure," Daisy replied, as her and the Ken doll followed Kat through the yard. "Let me tell you what I heard about Cris and my little cousin."

Katrina opened the barn door and waved for Daisy to stop talking. "I've already heard that story."

"About the puke?" Daisy asked.

"Yeah."

"And you're still banging him?"

Kat rolled her eyes and entered the barn hallway with the couple close behind.

Billy, Cris, and Beulah sat on the couch in front of the TV. The Professor was standing behind them, and a little girl in a sundress was seated with her arms crossed in the chair. Her tiny feet dangled as she looked impatiently around the room.

The Professor stepped out from behind the couch and stood by the TV. He motioned Kat and her friends over to some fold-out chairs.

"Take a seat, Kat. Everybody, take a seat," he said, pointing at the little girl in the chair. "This little girl is Dolly. Dolly, that pretty girl over there is Kat. That tough-looking girl next to her is Beulah's daughter, Daisy. And the pretty-boy is her boyfriend. I forget his name. It doesn't matter. The important thing is that we're all here."

"It's about time," Dolly said, glaring at Kat with her arms crossed. "Is this how you treat all of your clients?"

"Clients?" Daisy asked.

"Yes," the Professor said, addressing the room. "Some time ago, me and Billy had an idea."

"It was my idea, Albert," Billy said defiantly on the couch.

"Alright, fine," the Professor said. He adjusted his black top hat and continued. "Billy had the idea to begin a detective agency whereby we solve problems, answer riddles, and otherwise find solutions for a person's quandaries in exchange for their coinage."

"Why is he talking like that?" Daisy whispered to Kat.

"He thinks he's Abraham Lincoln," she whispered back before making eye contact with Cris on the couch. Both of them broke into a giggle fit.

"What is so funny?" asked the man in the top hat and lab coat.

"Nothing," Cris replied.

"As I was saying," the Professor continued, eyeing Cris suspiciously. "We never got this business venture off the ground before. But now, thanks to the talents of Miss Katrina Thompson, we have a second chance."

Cris started to applaud but his father gripped his wrist.

"Don't encourage him, son," Billy whispered.

"Now," the Professor continued, "Dolly here has agreed to pay us a total of five hundred dollars to find her missing brother. Beulah has agreed to pay us twenty dollars to find her beloved dog, Dirt Dobber.

We have all the information we need from Beulah on her case, but I wanted Dolly here to tell everyone what she told me about her brother. Are you ready, little girl?"

Dolly sighed and blurted out her story. "My younger brother, Micah, went missing about four days ago. He went with my dad to the nursing home and didn't come home with him. My daddy said he was staying with Grandpa for a while, but I don't believe him. I went to the police, and they came out to the place, but my dad told them the same thing and they just left and didn't do nothing. Two days ago, I went by the nursing home and asked to see my brother and they said he wasn't there. That's when I saw your card at the gas station and decided there was probably something paranormal going on."

Billy drank his beer and turned the volume up on the TV remote. "Is anyone else watching this shit?"

Everyone crowded in close to the television and watched the video footage of a sexy girl in a tight skirt smoking next to a dumpster in an alley outside a bar called *Beer & Teats*. The image on the screen blinked in and out of blackness several times and then a shadow formed on the top of the dumpster and grew into the outline of a tall, robed figure with the hood down.

The figure had the blurred face of a skeleton, and the empty eye sockets stared downward at the smoking girl. It wore a cloak that was as black as shadow with a hood that was ridiculously large. The hood was over twenty feet long and flowed down the side of the dumpster, extending to the other end of the alley.

"That's got to be fake, right?" asked Cris.

Everyone leaned in a little closer to the TV as the footage went to slow motion.

The creature threw the cowl upward with its bony hands and everything in its path was enveloped in darkness. The hood continued its journey over the top of the creature's head and then downward, engulfing the smoking girl and everything else in front of it. The entire screen went black for several slow-motion seconds until an empty alley faded back into existence. There was no girl, no cloaked skeleton, and no dumpster.

"What channel is this?" asked Daisy.

"It's the local news," Billy replied, pointing at the screen. "See, it's that reporter, what's her name?"

The video footage went away and a woman in a suit was holding a microphone next to two men in their early twenties. *The Ghost Raiders* was displayed on the screen below them and their names below that: *Charlie Hanson and Prince.*

One of the men was an average-looking geek. He was slightly overweight, wore thick glasses, and was currently in a pink Bigfoot t-shirt. The other guy was a tiny, dark-skinned man with sharp, surgically enhanced facial features. His hair glistened on the TV and he wore a purple, puffy shirt.

"And these are the investigators who filmed that disturbing footage," said the reporter. "Why don't you tell everyone who you are?"

"Charlie," the first man said, pushing his glasses up on his nose.

The second man was much bolder. He said his name proudly, tossing his product-filled mane of hair and speaking in a gentle but firm voice. "Prince. My name is Prince, and we're the Ghost Raiders."

"Who the hell is that?" asked Billy, turning down the volume on the TV.

"That is our competition," the Professor said before stepping behind the little girl in the chair. "Now turn that off and let's focus on our client. Dolly, why don't you tell them about the Boogeyman?"

The little girl put her head down and blew out a frustrated breath. "The Boogeyman had been coming in our room for a week or two before Micah disappeared. He came in through the window and told us that if we yelled he would kill Daddy and Mommy. So we kept quiet. He didn't do nothing but just sit on the floor between our beds. Sometimes he would whisper, but mostly he'd just sit there."

"What would he say?" asked Kat.

"Nothing much," the little girl said with her head still down. "Just a bunch of mumbling I couldn't understand, but Micah seemed to. My brother would sometimes talk back in the same mumbling way. He never told me what they said though. We never talked about the Boogeyman."

"Alright," the Professor said, placing a hand gently on the girl's shoulder. "Why don't you go on home now, Dolly?"

She got up and marched down the hall with her head down, slamming the barn door behind her.

Cris looked around and said, "Shouldn't someone drive her home or something? She is an eight-year-old, you know?"

"She'll be fine," replied the Professor. "Don't worry about Dolly. She is a strong little girl and her house is only a short walk through the woods."

Daisy spoke up first. "So what is this business called?"

"The Paranormal and Normal Investigators," Billy said. "Apparently Kat is head of advertising."

"Do you want me to join too?" asked Daisy.

"What about me?" asked Beulah.

The Professor held his chin and shook his head. "Not you. I'm sorry, Beulah, but you're already a client and that wouldn't be proper. It's unethical. If we ever need your help in the future, we'll give you some contract work or something."

Beulah whispered to Billy, "What's contract work?"

"It's paying you to do one single thing for us. Like whoring or being an assassin," Billy whispered back. "You get paid by the job."

"Oh, I like that," Beulah said, nodding her head. "I'll do it."

"Good," the Professor said, clapping his hands together and turning to Daisy. "Would you and Will like to work on contract too?"

"Maybe," Will replied. "It depends on how much you're paying."

"And how much shooting I get to do," Daisy said with a grin.

"Alright," continued the Professor. "That leaves Kat, Cris, Billy, and me. All four of us with equal shares, splitting everything four ways, minus any contract work of course. What do you say?"

The whole group looked around at each other and Cris raised his hand.

"Go ahead and speak, boy," the Professor said. "This isn't kindergarten."

"I was just wondering if anyone here has any actual detective skills? I know Dad was one a long time ago, but what happens when we run into something really dangerous? Like a criminal with a gun? Do we call the police or what?"

"No," Billy said. "No police, unless absolutely necessary. If we're hired to solve a mystery or save a damsel, we damned well better do it ourselves!"

"But won't that be dangerous?" asked Cris.

"Yes," said his dad. "Yes it will. We'll need to train you and Kat on how to shoot a weapon. I don't think Daisy will need any training. Ain't that right, Daisy?"

"Hell no," she said, putting her bulging arm around her boy toy. "Me and Will can shoot just fine."

"Well, then. Are there any more questions?" asked the Professor.

"What exactly is it that we'll be hired to do, again?" asked Daisy.

The Professor shrugged. "We'll investigate things for people. Solve their problems. Find missing persons and pets. I thought we went over that already."

"Do we fight crime? Like superheroes or something?" Will asked.

"Not exactly," Billy said. "We're a detective agency. Someone hires us to do a job and we do it. It's like whoring and assassinating. It's like I just told Beulah."

"We get it," said Daisy.

"I got a question," asked Kat. "What's gonna happen if the stuff like we just saw on the TV is actually real? What if the mystery we're solving turns out to be caused by something like that thing with the hood?"

"We kill it," said the Professor. "We are the Paranormal Investigators, aren't we?"

"How do you kill something like that?" Daisy asked.

"Oh, there are ways," the Professor said with a grin. "Pretty much anything can be killed."

"Really?" asked Katrina.

"Yup," said Billy. "There's always a way to kill, destroy, or otherwise trap supernatural things. Albert and I know all about the paranormal. We've been researching ghosts, demons, vampires, and all that shit forever. It's the one thing we have in common. After Rachel's funeral, we spent years doing nothing but studying..." He trailed off and pursed his lips.

"Studying that kind of shit," the Professor finished for him. "After my lovely sister died, we discovered our common interest. Suffice it to say, we have gathered a great deal of knowledge on things like what was on the TV just now."

"Who's Albert?" asked Daisy, getting no response.

"Well, what was it then?" asked Cris, crossing his arms defiantly. "What was that thing in the video footage that just ate the lady?"

The Professor stuck his chest out and replied, "There is a local, urban myth...a scary story that my mother told me and Billy's momma probably told him. It's about this hooded priest, and it's a horrifying story to tell a small child. The thing in that video looks like the evil thing from those children's stories. However, that video may have been nothing but a hoax. What are the odds that those two idiots on TV would have cameras up at just the right time and place to catch it? They could have heard of the story and set it up for publicity purposes.

"You see, it may be a blatant attempt by those two young fellows to get some customers. They're probably in the business of duping people. They scare people into thinking there's a scary ghost or ghoul and get people to pay them money. Then they put on a big dog and pony show and tell them the problem is fixed. It works most of the time too. If someone sees a ghost in their house and freaks out, they call someone like the Ghost Raiders. Now, the odds of them seeing a ghost twice in their lifetime are extremely low. Most people never see a real one at all. So, those two young gentlemen go into the house and put on a show and the client never sees a ghost again. It's the same thing with exorcisms. Most of the time, the spirit will leave the host voluntarily, or they were never there to begin with. So the priest just puts on a show and makes sure they're still around when the spirit is gone so they can get all the credit."

"So ghosts actually exist?" asked Kat.

"Why, of course," replied the Professor. "All kinds of things can exist. You exist, don't you?"

Katrina considered this and started to respond, before there was a loud knocking at the barn door. Everyone turned and waited for someone to go see who it was.

"I'll get it," Cris said, reluctantly getting up from his seat. "Maybe it's a ghost."

"None of you have ever seen a ghost?" asked the Professor. "A vampire? Or a fairy, maybe?"

"A fairy?" asked Beulah.

"Professor," began Will. "I don't think anyone here has seen anything supernatural before."

Billy laughed hysterically before wheezily talking through his beer. "Oh, you're all in for a lot of fun. A lot of fun."

"Is that a Ghost Raider?" asked Kat...and it was.

"This is Charlie and Prince from the TV," Cris said, pointing to the two young men standing beside him. "What a coincidence, right?"

"There are no coincidences," whispered the Professor.

"Hey, everybody," started Charlie. "We saw your website and everything, and, well..."

Charlie looked at his partner and Prince stepped forward, standing proudly in a purple suit and white-laced gloves.

"We need your help," he pleaded gently. "There's a monster on the loose and we need your help."

"Do you mean that thing on the news?" asked Kat. "That thing in the alley wasn't a hoax?"

"No," said Prince. "It's very real and we're going to murder the thing for what it did."

Charlie stepped forward, touching his friend's shoulder. "It's murdered a lot of people, including someone he loved very much and someone I cared for as well."

"Why don't you two boys sit down and have a beer?" Billy said, moving over on the couch to make room for them. "Just sit down and tell us what exactly that thing is."

"Yes," said the Professor. "Please tell us what's going on and maybe we can help."

So, the Ghost Raiders sat down on the couch and told everyone about the Priest of the Dark Pit.

Chapter 9

"ONCE UPON A TIME..." Charlie shrugged. "I guess that's how you start these things. Once there was this sorceress and she lived in a boat that perpetually floated on Lake Warren. The way the story's been passed down is that she floated on something more like a raft than a boat. It was just large enough for two people, and she sat on it day and night with a thing that came to be known as her son.

"Different stories say different things about the boy. Some say he was a twisted, hunchbacked child that she cradled in her arms, while others say that it was made of wood. Whatever the thing was, the story is that this witch spawned this child with a dark priest who was into demon worship and came from Europe sometime in the sixteenth century.

"Supposedly, this priest was the sole survivor of an expedition from Spain. The man wandered the forest alone and was on the very brink of starvation when he encountered a demon inside the trunk of a large tree. In exchange for his life, the priest renounced God and became the thing's disciple. He remained in the forest and wore only a dark robe made of smooth, blackened bark, woven by the demon itself.

"The indigenous people would tell future early American settlers this myth of a dark-robed white man who consorted with demons and lived with his witch in a black log cabin deep in the woods. They called him the Priest of the Dark Pit, because the man's hood was always up, and inside the hood where there should have been a face, there was only a deep abyss.

"Apparently, the story of that priest spread across the Southeastern part of the country up until the Civil War. During the war, some confederate soldiers wrote letters home, detailing the discovery by their company of a black log cabin with a naked, filthy, pregnant woman living inside. The soldiers, familiar with the folklore, chased the woman through the woods, but she disappeared and their bullets missed their mark. They never discovered her, but inside the cabin they found the corpse of an old man with a featureless face, just smooth flesh with slight indentions where the eyes and mouth should be. The old man's body was rotten, with maggots crawling over the bones and through the patchwork of broken flesh that still existed, but the holeless head was still fresh.

"The soldiers burned the evil cabin to the ground and had their chaplain consecrate the ashes. Tales of this destruction soon spread, but over time the myth was spoken of less and less, until the turn of the twentieth century when the first stories of the Lake Witch appeared.

"Sometime in the late 1890s, a hunter spotted the raft of black logs floating over the center of Lake Warren. There was a black-cloaked woman with her hood down, seated on the raft and holding a child. This was the Lake Witch, and there are more than a dozen different horrific stories attributed to her from this decade in history until she was said to have disappeared about fifteen years later.

"In the story of the hunter, he was driven crazy with visions of the woman and her strange child. According to this tale, the child was not a hunchback, but a loosely connected bundle of tiny sticks with a pebble for a head. The man told everyone that would listen about his dreams of being haunted by this wooden boy, and then one day the hunter was found floating in the lake, his mouth stuffed with splinters and his body poked full of tree limbs.

"This witch and her brood terrified the people that lived along this lake until the day she vanished. The vanishing began with a great wailing noise, and villagers from miles around came to the water's edge to see the Lake Witch crying and staring down at her covered up and swaddled baby. The wailing was said to have continued for an entire week. They shot at her with their guns and arrows, but no matter how they aimed, the shots would miss their mark. They were said to have waded out to the middle of the lake to drown the witch with their bare hands. However, no matter how furiously they moved through the water, the raft could not be reached. They sent their best swimmer out and he swam across the entire lake, but the raft would always be a safe distance away from him, no matter where he was in the water.

"On the seventh day, the witch's wailing suddenly stopped. The woman on the lake looked up from her child, which was something no one had ever seen the witch do outside of a dream, and pulled the cloak over her head. The hood grew in size as it fell forward, encompassing her face, the child, and eventually the entire raft. The bystanders reported seeing the darkness envelop the raft and the water around it in a matter of seconds, leaving a black, void-like crater in the surface of the lake which slowly faded away, resulting in ripples of water. The witch and her child were gone, vanishing under the hooded cloak.

"The Native Americans believed that she was the wife of the Priest of the Dark Pit, and that the raft was made from the remaining logs that survived the fire. They believed that after the priest's death, she took her child and went out upon the lake to grieve for fifty years, and on the fiftieth year she turned up her husband's cloak, and they vanished to look for him in the land of the dead.

"Since sometime after the Second World War, when this area started becoming more and more populated, there have been stories of a cloaked figure that swallowed up people inside a hood of death. Some older people tell stories of having seen the cloaked figure in and around the caves deep in the forests, and when someone goes missing there are whispers of the hooded monster. Some say it's the witch searching for her lover; others that it's the priest himself and that he made another deal with his demon. However, it was mostly a creepy campfire story and there weren't any believable eyewitness reports or anything until earlier this year.

"We heard about the first occurrences happening over the Christmas holidays. Someone called us up saying they watched their friend get devoured by an over-sized cloak walking home from a bar. Well, it sounded like some drunken fairy tale, but we took their money and said we would look into it. Then, a week later, some college kid came in with the same story. In the last five months, we've had twenty people contact us from all across the county and explain how they watched someone get devoured by this cloaked thing. We set up cameras in some alleys around town and got lucky when one of them actually recorded the creature taking a bartender. Then, two nights later, it ate both of our ex-girlfriends.

"We were going to see a psychic, who happened to be my ex-girlfriend, named Charlotte to see if she had noticed any changes around the town recently. Sometimes psychics can have intuitions about stuff, and we didn't know where else to turn. Prince brought his ex-girlfriend, Starla, too. She was always interested in weird stuff and wanted to tag along. We got there and immediately noticed something wasn't right. She knew we were coming over, but no one came to the door. I had a key, so the three of us went inside her house.

"As we walked in, the entire place got darker and darker until no one could see a thing. I was scrambling in the blackness trying to find the door when I ran into Prince. Somehow, the two of us found a wall, followed it to the front door, and opened it up. It was nighttime and there were streetlights outside and the moon was out, but as we stood on that front porch and looked back into the open doorway for Starla, both of us knew that no light could ever penetrate such an artificial blackness. Then, the darkness in the doorway faded and the inside of the house was visible again. Prince ran inside and I followed, but there was no trace of anyone.

"We made the mistake of going to the police. They threw us in a cell and thought we had something to do with the girl's disappearance. They let us go eventually, and we contacted the news with our supernatural video footage. They played it on TV, but we're not sure what good it did. Maybe some people will be scared enough not to go into the woods at night or down a dark alley alone, but it definitely isn't going to stop the thing.

"Prince found you online and, to be honest, you're the only other legitimate-looking group we could find that might believe us. We don't know if you can help destroy it. Hell, we don't even know if it can be killed. Both of us just wanted to communicate with you since we're kind of in the same line of work and everything. We thought that maybe, by some miracle, you might have an idea of how to kill it, since you investigate this stuff for a living."

"I got a question," Billy began. "Were you born with that name and have you always dressed like the 'Purple Rain' guy?"

Prince stuck his chest out proudly. "Born with the name, but adopted the fashion."

Billy shrugged. "Fair enough. Now, is this thing after you two, or did you just happen to be in the wrong place at the wrong time with those girls?"

"Don't know," answered Charlie. "I think it was a coincidence, but I'm not sure."

"There are no coincidences," whispered the Professor, a little too loudly.

"What was that?" asked Kat.

The Professor had been remembering more and more about the dream with Mr. Jenkins, and something, an intuition maybe, made him believe that the hooded creature was connected to him, to everything somehow. That the entire universe was part of an interconnected, invisible puppet string, and if you just tugged a little here and there you could create miracles out of thin air.

"You alright, Albert? You need a beer?" asked Billy, holding up a fresh one.

"Yes," the Professor said, rushing over and snatching it out of his brother-in-law's hand and popping the top.

"So, if it's not after you or anything," Kat said, "then you're just going after it for revenge or something?"

"Not just revenge," said Prince. "No one believes in it, so no one will be able to get rid of it. It'll just keep on killing folks if someone doesn't stop it. It could be my mother next, and I don't even want to think about that. It could be anyone going into those woods at night or leaving a restaurant in the city. Nobody is safe with that thing around."

"I'm sorry, Prince, but that's just stupid," Cris said from the couch. "We're not qualified to go running after a death machine like that. Maybe Daisy is, but it really seems like something for the Army, not people like us."

"I'm not getting swallowed up by no damned hood," said Daisy, grabbing her boyfriend's hand tightly, "and neither is my Will either."

"I'll do it," the Professor said, walking over and extending his hand to Charlie. "I'll help you kill the Dark Priest."

"Why don't you drink another beer, Albert?" Billy said.

"I'm fine," he replied, taking off his top hat and staring at it in his hands. "I don't know why, but I'm meant to do this, Billy. I've just got to do it."

"Well, what about our paying clients?" asked Katrina.

The Professor was still staring at his hat, trying to figure out why he had been wearing it in the first place.

"Professor?" Kat asked.

He looked up, startled. "Sorry. Um, why don't you and Cris do some surveillance on Dolly's dad? He was the last one to see the missing boy and he seems to be acting kind of strange. I don't know what Mr. Wright told the police to make them not start an investigation into a missing boy. There are a lot of missing kids right now, so it would seem weird for the police not to add him to the list."

"He works at that plant," Billy said. "I only seen him a few times before, but I can ask around."

Kat chimed in, "I can meet up with Cris one afternoon. We can go check out that grandfather and ask him some questions. Just message me after lunch and I'll meet up with you."

"Alright," Cris said.

"Do you need any contract work on this one, Mr. Professor?" Daisy asked.

"Yeah," Beulah leaned up. "I could use the money. I ain't doing no whoring though."

"Not yet," Albert answered, putting the top hat back on his head, "and it's just Professor. There is no mister or anything. We'll start working on Dolly's case tomorrow."

"What about Dirt Dobber?" asked Beulah.

Billy leaned over and grabbed her thigh. "Baby, I'm gonna find your dog. I'll start looking through every damn mound of fresh dirt I can find tomorrow. I promise."

"You better, or you won't be getting none from Beulah for a long time," she said, tossing his hand away and getting off the couch. "I'll want my twenty bucks back for that beer too. I got a headache with all this crazy shit talk. I'm going home."

Beulah left the barn.

Will lit up a joint, as he did just about every other hour of the day when he wasn't at work. He passed it to Daisy. Billy scooted over and made room as Kat squeezed onto the couch next to Cris.

The Professor watched the group of investigators gathered in his barn and wondered who was really behind this sudden spike in paranormal activity. He knew something nefarious was in motion, moving the entire town toward some awful conclusion, but he needed to find out whose spell it was in the first place.

"Professor?" asked Charlie.

"Hmmm?" the man in the lab coat said with a grin.

"If you're going to help us, let me show you something," Charlie said, pulling out his cell phone.

On the phone, the Professor watched as a video loaded and then played. It was the same video that had been on the local news earlier. The hood was going up, and everything was getting dark, and then...

"Right there," Charlie paused the video and enlarged a portion of it with his finger.

There, in the blackness of the hood, was a single, skinny strand of light where there should be no light at all.

Chapter 10

K AT WATCHED HER BOYFRIEND get out of the car and awkwardly walk toward her on the sidewalk.

"Have you heard from the Professor?" she asked.

"Nope," Cris said, giving her a peck on the lips. "I think he wasn't meeting up with those Ghost Raiders until closer to dark. You ready to interview the old timer?"

Kat grinned. "Yeah, let's go."

The Sunny Times Retirement Home was a large facility, but there was no security at the place, so they just walked right in. The cocky little girl had given them the room number of her grandfather. They exchanged an excited look as Cris knocked on the door of Room 122.

"Can I help you?" A young nurse appeared in the hallway. "Are you looking for Mr. Andrews?" she asked.

"Yes," Kat said. "We're related to him. Is he not in his room?"

"No. He's probably playing cards in the recreational room. I'll take you there, if you'll follow me." The nurse led them down the hall. "How are you related?"

"Through his son," Cris said. "Good old Uncle Terrence. We call the old man Pop-Pop. We love old Pop-Pop."

Kat pinched his ribs and they giggled. The teens followed the nurse around a corner and down another long hallway.

"Well, your Pop-Pop is a...lively old man," the nurse said. "We call him the Old Lobster around here. He's very affectionate. I've got the bruises on my butt cheeks to prove it."

At the end of the hallway was a large room. A group of retirees were playing cards at a table on one side. At another table, two old men played checkers, and in the back of the room on a leather couch there was an old couple making out.

"That's your Pop-Pop," the nurse said, pointing to the hot and heavy seniors. "He's a horny old thing."

She left and they walked over to the couch where the old man was dry-humping the elderly woman's leg.

"A-hem." Cris coughed into his hand. "Are you Pop... I mean, Mister Andrews?"

The man stopped humping, and somebody's great grandmother buttoned up her shirt and scurried away embarrassed.

"What's it to you?" said the old man, turning to face them and adjusting the slight bulge in his jeans. He had to be over eighty. Disgusting gray hair sprouted from his button-down shirt tucked into a pair of jeans, and his jeans tucked into a pair of black cowboy boots.

"Your granddaughter, Dolly, sent us," began Kat. "She hired us to find your grandson, Micah. It seems that he disappeared after leaving this place last week."

The old man leaned forward on the couch. "You got a cigarette?"

"No," Cris said. "We don't smoke, sorry."

The man pursed his lips. "So the little brat's still missing?"

"Yes," Kat said. "Did you know he was gone?"

"Of course. He's my grandson, ain't he?" the old man said. "I just assumed they found the little pecker by now. Well, what do you want with me?"

"We just want to ask you a few questions," Kat began. "Do you mind?"

The old man reached out and gently touched her hand.

"Not if you're the one asking them, angel." The man winked. "Go right ahead."

Kat's eyes fell to the boner trying to escape his jeans and then came up again to meet the old man's gaze, a gaze that was far too proud to be embarrassed.

She tugged her hand away slowly, trying to be as polite as possible. "Well, did you see anything weird that day, Mr. Andrews? Was your son acting strange? Anything you can tell us would help."

"Nope. I don't remember anything really, but that's not my son. Terrence is my son-in-law. He may be banging my daughter, but that don't make him my progeny."

"The boy went missing when he left here, sir," Cris said. "Are you sure you didn't see anything unusual during their visit?"

"I have been seeing my wife a lot more lately," the man began. "She's dead, but I can still see her sometimes, and the last two weeks I've seen her just about every night. But as for little Micah, there was nothing unusual about the visit. He stayed for about fifteen minutes and then left. Their dad brings them up here every so often and they stay about fifteen or twenty minutes and then he makes them leave."

Cris noticed something in the garden of gray chest hairs. Muddled in the mess on the old man's chest was a strange-looking medallion.

"What's that around your neck?" Cris asked.

Mr. Andrews pulled the chain up and looked lovingly at the squishy, glistening medallion on the end of it. It was puffy and had the letter "A" with a snake winding through it. "Oh, that's some jewelry I stole from my daughter's room last month. I was going to sell it, but to be honest, the ladies love it. It's the damnedest thing how it looks all flesh-colored and it stays kind of soft all the time. I don't know why she had it."

The old man looked up from the necklace with a serious look on his face. "I'll tell you one thing. That Terrence is not a nice fellow. That's for damn sure. That day, and every time he brought them kids up here, both the little girl and the little pecker were scared to death of him. Don't ask me why. I never seen him hurt no one or yell at those kids or anything, but you can tell when a child is scared of an adult, and those kids have been scared of him for months."

"How about before that?" asked Kat.

"No. I just noticed it the last few months."

"Thank you, Mister Andrews," Cris said, shaking the man's hand. "We really appreciate your time."

The old man gripped Cris's hand tightly. "You sure you don't have no cigarettes?"

Cris shook his head no.

"Goodbye, Mr. Andrews," Kat said, putting a business card in his shirt pocket. "Call us if you think of anything else."

Cris got his hand back and followed her out of the room. The dirty old man licked his lips and watched them both from behind.

"Is he still watching?" Cris asked as they moved briskly down the hallway.

"Yes," Kat said, turning slightly to look. "That was disgusting. He stared at my tits the whole time."

"I thought he was going to rape me or something."

They turned the corner and were out of the old man's vision.

"I gotta go to the bathroom," Kat said. "Wait here a minute."

"I'll call Billy and let him know what happened."

As Katrina went into the bathroom, Cris put the cell phone to his ear.

"Hello, boy," came Billy's voice over the phone.

"Hey. We saw the grandfather. Turns out he's a horny old man."

"Most are nowadays."

"He said the boy had been scared of Terrence," Cris said. "Maybe the father did something to him."

"Maybe."

"Also, the man had a necklace with a soft, disgusting medallion on the end of it. He stole it from his daughter. It had the letter A with some snakes on it. It was kind of strange."

"The giant serpent," Billy muttered.

Kat came out of the bathroom to see an alarmed look on Cris's face.

"Huh?" Cris asked. "What are you talking about?"

"You ever heard of Apep?" Billy asked. "No, I guess not. Well, let me go through the CliffsNotes for you. Apep is a name that's been used for a particular kind of demon or demi-god sometimes. The mythology came from North Africa long ago. It was really popular thousands of years ago, but through the years different cults of Apep have still popped up from time to time. That medallion is the symbol for the thing, which means that Mr. Andrews' daughter must be a fan."

"They worship it? What does that have to do with the missing boy?" asked Cris.

"Worship what?" asked Kat, and her boyfriend politely hushed her.

"I don't know," continued Billy. "You asked about the serpent demon and I told you. It was a big cult in Egyptian times. It's basically a powerful entity that takes the form of a giant reptilian creature. Stories were written of conjurers that would summon Apep into this world, and if that's what is going on here, then we got a much bigger problem than one missing boy."

"Is that something that can actually be done?" Cris asked in a trembling voice. "I mean, demons don't actually exist, do they?"

"Oh, they exist alright, son," Billy said. "Believe me, they exist, but they're not really a problem normally. I mean, warlocks conjure demons to this side sometimes to ask questions and gain knowledge and stuff like that. Shit happens, you know? But usually not things like Apep. A single warlock shouldn't do that. No sane person would summon it. The old cults of Apep were like your modern-day anarchists, they wanted the serpent summoned so that it would destroy everything."

"Couldn't the horny man's daughter just be a member of the cult?" asked Cris. "That doesn't mean that they're trying to summon the thing, right?"

"Members of a cult like that usually only have one purpose in mind. If it has any sort of a following right now, then that could mean trouble. It's said that one who wears the medallion of Apep can hear the whispers of the serpent's acolytes. These devout followers can possess a human host and bring forth their dark lord. Once summoned, the serpent god is supposed to hasten the end of times, kind of like the Anti-Christ or something, if the Anti-Christ was a snake. Some writings say that the creature carries a plague and can raise an army of dead things and creatures that aren't dead but should be."

Cris followed Kat out of the retirement home and into the parking lot, talking as he went. "Assuming you're not insane, then how do they summon the thing?"

"It's not summoned from out of nowhere. Things that powerful never really go away altogether. Those types of creatures—dark entities, that is—just lie hidden until an opportunity appears, or until they get bored or something. The necklace is made from a sacrifice to the deity. When the acolytes make the sacrifice, then medallions are formed out of the innards."

"Did you just say innards?" Cris asked.

"Yes. It's supposed to be made from intestines," Billy said. "It could be a dog or rabbit, but it could be human too. Whatever the deity desires. If you saw the necklace, then someone made it. That means that the demon's minions are among us and he's got a following going too."

"I don't know if it was an innards necklace or not," Cris muttered. "I didn't get that good a look at the thing."

"Well, assuming that one of Apep's helpers have already taken possession of a human host, then it is probably using that person to build up a cult to go out and do one of them human sacrifices in the woods-type things." Billy whistled through the phone. "If they actually get it to appear, then the great serpent could be protected by its cult members until eventually it feels strong enough to come out of hiding and into our world to bring chaos and destruction. Assuming it is summoned, I would think it would want to get a pretty good following going before it came out of hiding. But if it can really mind-control people like the stories say, then it could make a cult out of everyone in town if it wanted to. Would that still make it a cult if everyone were a member?"

"Yes," Cris said, getting into Kat's car. "That definitely still sounds like a cult. Well, it was nice talking to you. Thanks for the information. Why don't you go do some work now?"

"Is that a joke?"

"Bye, Dad."

Cris hung up. As Katrina drove them to Terrence's house for a stakeout, he told her the CliffsNotes version of Apep the serpent God.

"What do you think?" he asked. "Is my dad crazy?"

"I don't know," Kat said. "I haven't seen proof of anything super-natural yet, other than that video those two guys had which could've been a fake."

"Yeah," Cris said. "It's going to be difficult for me to believe in something like that just because of some necklace. I need more proof."

"Me too," Kat said, pulling to a stop on the side of the road. "Well, we're here. That's his house. What do we do now?"

Cris shrugged. "I guess we look for a giant snake."

Kat switched off the engine and turned to face him. "From what the old man said, that little pecker was scared of Terrence. Maybe he's the one stealing all the kids after all. Maybe he's sacrificing them in the woods or something like that."

"Maybe," Cris said, brushing aside her hair. "You want to make out?"

"Sure."

The sun was starting to go down, but there was still enough light for them to have seen Terrence walk out the door and into the front yard. However, they were too busy fooling around to notice. They never saw his yellow eyes blazing in their direction as he disappeared around the side of the house and into the woods that bordered the back yard. They also didn't notice the next-door neighbor, an elderly widow named Miss Jameson, when she stumbled out her front door like a zombie and marched as if she were sleepwalking around the side of Terrence's house...and they didn't see the mass of large snakes that followed her either.

Chapter 11

"ARE YOU SURE ABOUT this?" Charlie asked, leaning against a slide that was only slightly taller than him.

"Yes. I'm sure," said the Professor.

The sun was setting behind the trees and they were standing in the playground of an elementary school.

The Professor sat down on a swing set and swayed back and forth. "I don't know how, but I just know that this is where the monster will appear. I don't know if the voice told me this information or not, but...when the child speaks to me it sounds like gibberish, but somehow my brain understands it and I just remember things."

"Have you always heard voices in there?" asked Charlie, sitting on one of the swings.

The Professor sighed. "For as long as I can remember. But this child's voice is new. I've been remembering more and more things since this morning too. Things that I thought had been dreams but now I'm not so sure. I can remember talking to the cave child now, and I can't explain why or how, but sometimes the boy whispers helpful information to me and other times I just know things, as if he's whispered it before. Maybe he visits me in dreams, I don't know."

"It's pretty weird," Charlie said.

"I know!" the wild-eyed man in the lab coat said. "Not only that, but somehow I know what he's telling me is the truth. He called me a wizard. Can you believe that?"

"Are you one?"

The Professor shrugged. "I don't know. The boy was talking about wizard schools too. Have you ever heard of anything as stupid as that?"

"Actually, yes. Supposedly, there's some famous school of magic in England that's not called Hogwarts. It's kind of got an underground following since no one can ever find it, but they have a website. Prince went looking for it when he was younger. He went with some group. They traveled all across that English countryside, and he said they never saw any sign of it."

"Why do you people think it exists if no one's ever seen it?" asked the Professor.

"Well, they've got a website," Charlie said, shrugging. "Also, there are people who say they've been there. Not many people believe them, of course. There's supposed to be one out on the West Coast too."

"That's what the boy told me," the Professor said. "I remember now. He said he was going away to wizard school in Portland, or it might have been San Diego. Either way, he said something about helping me get in if I wanted to."

"You should. You would make a good wizard."

"You think so?"

"Oh, here he comes," Charlie said. "I hope he brought my chainsaw."

Prince approached them wearing a fluffy, laced shirt and tight purple pants. He gingerly carried a small, muddy chainsaw. He passed the weapon to Charlie, pulled some hand lotion out of his pants, and rubbed it between his palms.

"Is my stuff in the backpack?" asked the Professor from the swing.

"Yeah," Prince said softly. He unzipped the backpack and handed a wooden cross about six inches tall to the Professor.

"I still don't know what you're going to do with that," Charlie said. "The thing's not a vampire."

The Professor shrugged. "It was the first thing that came to mind. Prince, did you bring anything?"

The dainty man pulled out a flask and took a swig. "Vodka and apple juice. Want some?"

"Sure," the Professor said, taking a drink and handing it to Charlie. "What are you going to do with that chainsaw?"

"Separate the hood," Charlie took a swig from the flask, "from the cloak. If it's real, then we should be able to cut it, right?"

"Smart," the Professor said, eyeing the wooden cross suspiciously and swinging lightly back and forth. "That's pretty smart thinking. I just hope that weird little boy knows what I'm doing."

"Me too," said Charlie, adjusting the chain on his saw. "Maybe if he's telling you to be here tonight, then he's got a plan. You never know."

The Professor put the cross on his lap and grabbed hold of the chains to swing a little higher while he spoke. "Back in that cave, the boy said he needed to take something from me in order to do a spell that would take care of this hooded creature and some other monster before he went off to school. That was one reason for bringing me out there in the first place."

"Do you remember what he took?" Prince asked gently.

"No," the Professor answered, shaking his head. "I can't remember him taking anything. I do recall him telling me that I wouldn't miss it though. He said that I wouldn't even miss it. He was right too. I don't miss whatever it was that he took."

"So, let me get this straight," Prince said. "We're just going to wait around in this playground all night for a monster to appear, and then hope that this little kid from your dreams or whatever has a plan to destroy the thing before it murders all of us?"

The Professor stopped swinging long enough to nod his head. "That sounds about right to me. Only I'll be the one to destroy it, or one of us at least, not the boy. He kind of set it all up when he cast the spell."

"You alright with this, Charlie?" Prince asked his friend.

"You got any better ideas?" Charlie asked. "Besides, if it turns out that he's crazy, then that thing won't appear anyway and we can go home in the morning."

"I can hear you, you know," the Professor said.

He rocked forward and back on the swing, reconsidering all the possible connections between that glowing strand of light in the video and the Jenkins boy. He replayed in his mind how the child had plucked the luminous tendrils from his own head. He had only run into that boy a few times in the park before and nothing had ever indicated he was a wizard. He remembered the father too. How he used to wander off into the woods like the boy, but who would have thought a whole family of magicians lived in that trailer park?

Albert had always been afraid of heights, but as he swung higher and higher, the man now found that it wasn't all that bad. He swung back and forth, his two companions watching him fly through the air. The swing poles rattled around him as the Professor used his weight to go as high above the ground as the thing would reach. At the very peak of his swing, the man looked down and realized that he was not even remotely afraid.

The three of them were getting tipsy by the time it got dark, and were a little drunk when the Priest of the Dark Pit finally appeared. It was just after ten and they were swaying lightly on the swinging seats designed for tiny children. Full dark had settled in, and it had been eerily quiet for the past hour. The men were seated inches apart, but as far away as could be in their minds. Their brains swam in vodka and apple juice, with each person deep in contemplation as they swung in the darkness.

Prince was re-living the dinner from six months earlier, the night Starla had broken up with him. She had insisted on paying for her own meal and he remembered fingering the little black jewelry box in his front pants pocket while she flagged down the waiter. For months after that, he had beaten himself up for not being rougher with her, the way a real man would have...a man like Freddy Tacklebox.

Fred Tacklebox sure wouldn't have stood for her splitting the check. He would have insisted to the point of waving the waiter down himself, and Prince hadn't even lifted a hand. He had been too scared to make her upset. Back in high school, Freddy had always purposefully gone out of his way to upset the women he dated, and they probably never dumped him at a fancy restaurant either.

Starla rebounded right into Freddy, and she would've been Mrs. Tacklebox by now if her ex-boyfriend hadn't let her die. It seemed that Prince was always letting people he loved down. He sighed and fantasized about the dream wedding that had been replayed in his mind over a hundred times. There was Starla walking down the aisle in a puffy purple dress and pink tennis shoes; and him all newly mustached, afroed, and shirtless, wearing only a scarf and his lucky leather pants; and the caged, cooing white doves at the back of the church just waiting to be set free.

Charlie was dreaming too. His mind conjured visions of the imaginary angel that sometimes whispered in his head at night. His guardian angel, Ariel, had spoken to him in whispers since he was a kid. He hadn't heard from Ariel in months and was beginning to wonder if he may be as crazy as the old wizard on the swing next to him.

The Professor was trying to focus on pushing imaginary strings and strands of light out of his brain, but found that it was too much like trying to do the breathing correct in a yoga pose. He gave up and thought of nothing much at all. Just as he was beginning to get bored again, the Professor heard the creature's voice and felt its rancid breath on the back of his neck.

Hello, wizard.

He sprang from the swing and turned to see the hooded priest less than a car-length away. It looked like a robe with skeleton hands. Inside that hood was a black pit that made the Professor shudder, but he couldn't stop looking. He took a step forward before breaking the trance and standing his ground.

The two young men turned in their swings to gaze into the faceless void. A few seconds passed where nobody moved. Then there was a rumble of thunder from somewhere far away, and Albert looked up to see a star-filled sky, as clear as any he could recall. Then another roar of thunder that seemed to come from a galaxy far away, and the ground shook underneath them.

All of this lasted about five seconds, and the hooded thing never moved. When the shaking lessened, the two ghost hunters rushed forward. Charlie raised the chainsaw high above his head before lowering it with a confused look on his face, mouthing something inaudible just as the ground stopped shaking and the world around them went silent.

Everything was engulfed in darkness, and it happened so quickly that the Professor almost forgot that there had been any stars at all. It was like waking too fast from a nightmare and not knowing what parts had been real or fantasy. When he became oriented in this blackness, he remembered the roaring of thunder and the trembling earth, and realized how absolutely silent it had become.

There was no ground either.

He was floating inside a bleak, dark space.

A few silent seconds passed before there were sounds once again...and then light as well. His sight slowly recovered. The Professor saw that he was seated on a soft, gyrating, foul-smelling bodily organ of enormous proportions. It reminded him of a human liver even though it was larger than a house. He felt himself rising and falling with the pulsing organ, and his entire body was dripping with clear-colored goo.

His head turned to see the glistening walls undulating dizzily around him, and the sounds of a heartbeat from somewhere black that looked like a tunnel. He saw Charlie's head with eyes wide open, but no matter how hard he looked, there was no body. There was only the head.

After surveying the room and looking down at his legs, he reached three conclusions.

He was alone.

He was in the belly of the beastly thing.

And after seeing how much of his blood was on the floor beneath him, Albert knew that he was dying.

While the Professor sat in darkness, Prince was busy sprinting down the suburban sidewalks. Completely oblivious to the approaching sirens, he was tackled by something he assumed to be a goblin or another sort of monster the way the night had gone so far. However, it turned out to be Officer Freddy Tacklebox. The blow knocked the breath out of the little man and he moaned on the sidewalk as the officer flipped him over and roughly cuffed his tiny wrists.

"Hey!" yelled Prince. "What are you doing, Freddy?"

"You have the right to remain silent," Officer Tacklebox said, lifting him off the ground as the police cars came roaring down the street. "Aw shit, little buddy. I'll finish reading your rights on the way to the station. Why did you do it? I just don't understand why you'd go and do something like that. Was it because of Starla? I understand if it was. I miss her too, you know. Her just up and disappearing like that was strange, but I like to think she's just out on one of her adventures and maybe when it's all over she'll come back home."

"Do what? What did I do?" Prince asked, licking the blood from his lip and wondering why there were five police cars blocking the road, all the cops pointing their guns at him.

"What did you do? You cut his head off, little buddy," Freddy continued. "I thought Charlie was your friend. Why would you do something like that?"

"Charlie? Is he alright?"

The officer shook his head and dragged the man into the backseat of a police vehicle. "Come on then. I guess you're in some kind of psycho-shock or something. I just don't understand it, that's all."

The car door slammed and Prince peered through it at all the police officers glaring with contempt and it hit him all at once that Charlie was dead. That meant that the man he loved, his only real friend in the world, was gone. Prince wiped the tears from his face.

Freddy got into the front seat and drove away.

"You crying?" the officer asked, looking in the rearview mirror. "Just tell me where you put the head, little buddy. If you do that, they might not give you the chair."

"I didn't kill him," Prince muttered.

"Sure," the officer said soothingly. "Sure thing, little buddy. Want me to read you your rights now?"

"I don't care."

As the officer read off the suspect's legal rights from memory, Prince remembered the last time he had seen his friend alive. Charlie had lifted up the chainsaw and then the world went silent and dark, and Prince had run away.

He recalled peeking over his shoulder after getting across the street from the playground, right before breaking into a full-out sprint down the sidewalk, and seeing nothing there. There was no darkness, no silence, no hooded priest, and no Charlie.

He had kept running and hadn't looked back again until Freddy tackled and cuffed him. How had the police gotten there so quickly? He hadn't been running for long before he was tackled. Prince squinted through the caged barrier at the digital clock on the console. It had been three hours since he had last seen Charlie alive.

Chapter 12

KAT PARKED ON THE side of the road and rolled down her window as Buddy approached. He was shirtless in his white Wranglers and SECURITY ball cap.

"Good evening, children," Buddy said, leaning into the car window. "Nothing to see here. Miss Stoddard's just got everybody riled up, but they're getting calmed down now and will be dispersing momentarily."

Cris leaned his head forward to see across the drive. "I'm old enough to vote, you know."

"Yeah," Kat insisted, with both hands on the wheel. "We're not children, Buddy. What's going on here anyway?"

Up ahead, a crowd of about two dozen people gathered on the lawn of a trailer, with a very large Miss Stoddard standing alone at the head of them. A uniformed policewoman was on the porch glaring across the yard with her arms crossed and her head shaking back and forth. The preacher stood next to her in an I HEART JESUS hat and an old thrift store suit.

"The Stoddards want to dish out some street justice. They're convinced that one of those pedophiles the preacher keeps back there," Buddy pointed to the three nasty campers behind the trailer, "is responsible for the missing children. By the way, what were you doing over at Terrence's earlier tonight?"

"How did you know we were over there?" Kat asked.

"Well, I've been following him for a while now myself. He's been acting weird the last few months, going into the woods all the time for no good reason, looking at butts in the Walmart, and then his little boy went missing. So I figure he may have something to do with the missing children. Now, what are you watching his house for?"

"Same thing," Kat said. "Except we're getting paid to do it. We're private investigators now, Buddy. Someone hired us to find that boy. We think Terrence had something to do with it too."

Buddy scratched his balls and then his head in confusion. "You children don't need to be messed up in something like that. Terrence is dangerous. I've been watching him and there's something bad going on."

"Like what?" Kat asked.

"I can't tell you that. It's confidential. Only me and the rest of the security team can know about it."

"You mean Ralph?" asked Cris.

"Pretty much, but I haven't even told him anything yet," Buddy said. "I've been keeping it all hush-hush until I've got enough evidence to arrest him myself."

"You can't arrest him, Buddy," Kat said. "Neither can we. Only the real police can do that. What is so dangerous about Terrence anyway?"

"Alright, if I tell you, will you promise not to tell anybody?"

"Promise," the teenagers said at the same time.

"Well, I've seen him go into the woods at night with a bunch of other people. They all go to this clearing way out deep in the forest, somewhere that I never even knew existed. They all just stare at this tree and talk to themselves. It's mostly the neighbors, but recently the crowd's gotten bigger."

"What's so dangerous about that?" asked Cris.

"It's just a gut feeling, is all," Buddy said, rubbing his bare belly. "Plus, there's always a bunch of snakes in that part of the woods, really big and poisonous ones. They look like rattlesnakes, and if you go out there following him then you might get bit. Then both your daddies would be upset with me for telling you about it in the first place. Part of my job is to keep children like you out of danger."

"Snakes, huh?" Kat said, getting out of the car. "Well, you can't keep us from stalking Terrence. It's a free country."

"Yeah, maybe it is," Buddy said.

"You gonna tuck us children in later too?" Cris asked, getting out of the vehicle and following Kat toward the crowd.

Buddy scowled in their direction. His tummy growled and he rubbed his belly again as Ralph approached from the crowd.

"Just talked to Turner," Ralph said. "She says they ain't going to arrest nobody out here today. She says they ain't got no cause to arrest them molesters. She says that the preacher won't let her look in them campers either."

"Well, of course not," Buddy said. "Police can't go in them campers without a warrant. Everybody knows that. How about Stoddard? She calm down yet?"

"Nope," Ralph said, rubbing his belly through the camouflaged t-shirt tucked into his black Wranglers. "She's got that bunch too excited. They'll be back, you can be sure of that. She organized a meeting in the community center on Tuesday night. She's the president of the watch now and will probably be handing out guns and ammo to everyone."

"They're gonna end up killing Brother Pruitt," Buddy said, shaking his head and giving his belly a firm pat. "What time does it start?"

"Seven," Ralph said.

Buddy nodded and watched the crowd.

Kat had shoved her way through the spectators.

"What on earth are you doing here?" Kat's father asked, spotting his daughter approaching.

"Watching the show," Kat said. "Dad, you know Cris, don't you?"

Her father stuck his hand out to shake. "Of course. You're Billy's son, aren't you?"

Cris shook it firmly. "Yes, sir. But I'm nothing like him. I promise."

"Good," Mr. Thompson replied. "Now, why don't the two of you get out of here? That crazy Stoddard family is liable to start shooting up the place."

"Alright. I'll see you at home later," Kat said, giving her dad a hug and grabbing Cris's hand to lead him away.

Cris flashed his free hand up to wave goodbye. "Goodbye, Mr. Thompson."

Kat's father didn't wave back. He just stared at the couple for a moment with a concerned look on his face and both hands on his hips. He turned to the crowd just as the officer shushed everyone.

"Alright, listen up," Officer Caitlin Turner screamed over the noise. "I want everybody off the preacher's property right now. You got five minutes and then I start putting handcuffs on trespassers and arresting folks, starting with anyone whose last name is Stoddard."

Miss Stoddard nodded to the crowd and ushered them to their vehicles. Her two sons, both almost as large as their mother, helped her into the passenger seat of a humongous truck with five-foot-tall wheels. She leaned out the window as one of the boys got in the bed and the other got behind the wheel.

"We'll be back, Officer Lady," she yelled in a baritone voice out the window. The truck rumbled to a start and the wheels spun dirt all over the car parked behind it as she yelled over the roaring engine.

"Tomorrow night, Preacher. We'll dish out our own justice tomorrow night!"

Kat hurried into her car and rolled up the window as Miss Stoddard's voice trailed off. She smiled across the console and started the car.

"What?" asked Cris.

Kat tapped the corner of her mouth with an index finger and Cris rubbed his in response.

"What is it? Did I get it?" he asked, still brushing and pursing his lip.

Kat's cheeks were read. "You got it. It was just lipstick."

Cris smiled back and wiped it off. "Oh. You think your dad saw it?

"Maybe," Kat said, pulling onto the main road.

Chapter 13

The Professor stood next to the severed head and pressed one hand over the open gash in his thigh. Blood flowed down both legs, and on the floor was a puddle that should have killed him by now.

The blood kept pouring until there was enough to drown a tiny infant. However, when the bulk of the gushing was over, somehow he was still alive.

Sure, there was a headache and his arms were whiter than a newly-wed's picket fence, but he really didn't feel all that bad. He considered that maybe the rules of death didn't apply inside this hooded thing, but one look at poor Charlie's head killed that hypothesis. He just shrugged and figured that, at the moment, it wasn't really that important why it was occurring. The Professor was alive and inside another living organism, and he needed to find a way out.

He picked up the chainsaw and looked around, trying to decide where to stick it. The walls were wet and slick. Cutting through them might get him out. He had no idea where he really was inside the thing and decided to take a walk.

In the next chamber, he passed by a giant pile of bones and came to an incline. He ascended it only to find other slants, and even some steps, all of which led him farther upward. After a long walk, he entered a chamber with two gigantic interconnected tubes on either side of him. They contained something that looked similar to human lungs, if the human using them was fifty feet tall. The tubes were filled with a thick, clear liquid that the lungs swished around in.

He deduced that this must be the thing's chest, but couldn't hear a heartbeat. The Professor wondered if the creature might not have a heart at all. The man yanked on the starter rope and the saw roared to life. He pushed the blade against the container, and after a few moments the container cracked, and he was sawing through the fleshy lung.

After both lungs were cut in half, he approached an icky wall and stuck it with the saw. The Professor shook as it cut through the exterior of the monster, and he fell forward a little as the blade found emptiness on the other side. Grinning, he pushed hard on the roaring saw, cutting out a horizontal, oval-shaped hole through which he saw the stars shining on Lake Warren.

The Professor kept cutting. He cut the hole larger and larger until it was big enough to fit several people through. Then, in a burst of enthusiasm and hubris, the man leaped out.

Covered in goo, he released a primal warrior's scream all the way down with the chainsaw held above his head. The drop was a little farther than he thought. His legs shattered on impact and became a mangled mess of protruding bone and meat on the muddy ground...and he was vibrating. The turning saw blade poked out of Albert's midsection, shaking his entire body.

He reached with a vibrating hand and flipped off the saw. His body suddenly went still and felt like it weighed a thousand pounds. He heard someone crying and thought it was him. All he wanted to do was go to sleep.

The Professor lazily gazed down at the now-stilled saw sticking out of him, and then turned to see the hooded creature on its knees by the shores of the lake. The sobs were coming from inside that gigantic hood, but he couldn't see anything but void within. The cloaked figure was on its knees and the top of the hood was a good twenty feet or more off the ground. The creature was vanishing slowly, fading into nothingness right before his eyes.

There was no pain in the Professor's crumpled mess of a body, and he was still alive for some reason. Too sleepy to move anything but his head, he kept his eyes open long enough to watch the sobbing hood slowly go from a solid thing of this world to a translucent ghost, then to a mere formation of mist that drifted over the water and fell with a quiet ripple. The sobbing continued for a few seconds more, and then the ripple was gone as well. Apparently, even the Priest of the Dark Pit feared death.

He wouldn't let me stay without the deaths. After all that searching, I never found my son. How did you do it, Wizard?

The voice was scratchy and deep. It echoed in the Professor's head and he somehow spoke back in kind.

I'm not a real wizard, the Professor communicated with eyes now closed, beginning to drift in darkness outside of his own body...thinking he was finally going to die.

I never expected to encounter, much less eat, an immortal human.

The Professor was swimming in the darkness when he responded.

But I'm dying right now.

That God-boy, the dissipating creature echoed. *Did he create you as well?*

No. What did he take from me?

I see now. It is the boy's spell.

What did he remove?

You really do not know?

No.

The swirling nothingness grew still and the Professor was no longer moving through it as the creature answered.

He took your mortality. I was done the moment your deathless vessel infected me.

But I'm dying right now. I can see a light. I can see a light.

Go to that light, Wizard. Go to the light.

The Professor awoke in his recliner, wearing his lab coat, in his secret room where he kept his most secret things. He wiped some eye gunk on his shirtsleeve and felt his legs to make sure they were intact...and to his surprise, they were.

All four walls in his secret room were covered with bookcases. Though most of the shelves were filled with books, a few rows were filled with something else entirely. They held floating heads of all manner of creatures encased in a ball of glass filled with a clear liquid. Each glass container had a dead face in the center, and if someone shook it, they might expect snow to fly around inside.

They were monstrous faces of otherworldly things. In one was the shrunken head of a troll. In another was a stone golem's head. One had the head of a rabbit that looked far too human to have just been a rabbit. There were dozens of these monstrosities, but the Professor paid them no attention. His mind was wholly concerned with why he wasn't dead and how he had gotten back to the barn.

He paced over and over his Bigfoot rug for what must have been an hour, and then looked at the cuckoo clock. The bird waddled out and opened its tiny mouth, but made no sound. Billy had cut out the wooden tongue years ago, but never mind that now.

The Professor needed to think!

A long, hot shower should do it. He came up with a lot of his ideas in the shower. He took off his shoes and walked out of the room, crossing the empty barn to the bathroom. As he walked, the Professor considered the timeline of events.

- Sometime before midnight, he was devoured by the darkness in that hooded thing.

- Then he cut his way out, emerging by the lake before the sun came up.

- He was now in the barn at eight o'clock in the morning.

He had bled out inside the creature. Then he broke his legs, and then there was the chainsaw blade churning through his guts and shaking his entire constitution. He remembered thinking death would never take him, but then there was the sleepiness, and then the darkness, and finally the bright light. The bright light meant he should be dead. That was Dying 101, right?

Why had the light led me here, unharmed in the barn?

He opened the bathroom door and remembered what the priest had said about his mortality.

Could it be true? Do people even have something called mortality inside them?

Perhaps the thing had meant the spirit, which meant he no longer had a soul.

Did this mean I really was immortal?

His thoughts elsewhere, the Professor never saw how slick the tiled bathroom floor actually was. There were puddles of standing water, and when his dirty sock slipped on the wet tile, the old man's legs flew out in front of him and he went airborne.

His body floated horizontally toward the commode and his legs landed on top of it first, then the back of his head raced toward the floor, smacking hard on the tile. His vision blurred, but he could see the blood forming next to his head...and then the darkness...and then the light...and then he bolted upright in his favorite recliner.

He felt his head and there was no blood. No bruises either. The cuckoo clock said it was almost nine in the morning. The Professor left his secret room and stormed through the barn, opening up the bathroom door.

There was no standing water.

There was no pool of blood. There was no blood at all.

He was confused when a hand landed on his shoulder, making him jump a few inches off the ground and whirl around before his feet touched the tile again.

"Whoa!" Billy said, retracting his hand and stepping back. "Didn't mean to startle you. You alright?"

"No," the Professor said, eyes closed and head shaking. "No, I'm not alright. I should be dead. Don't you understand? I should be dead!"

"Dead? What are you talking about, Albert?"

"Oh, I don't know," he responded, before shoving past his brother-in-law. "Just don't bother me for a few hours. I'm going to be running some experiments."

He stormed across the barn, opened the door with the big DO NOT ENTER sign on it, and slammed it shut.

"You need any help?" Billy yelled.

"No!" came the response from behind the door.

In the secret room, the Professor searched for a drawer and then rustled through a large red chest in the corner. He threw various objects onto the huge rug with the ape-like head on one end of it. Littering the carcass were a dull-bladed machete, a straight razor, a large baggie of marijuana, a thick hardcover book (it was over two thousand pages and he'd never opened it before; he mainly kept it for decoration), and a long, thick extension cord.

He stood over the rug and considered the objects. Then he picked up the extension cord and tied a knot with enough room in the noose for a human head. The Professor looked around for a place to hang. Nothing. He shrugged and grabbed a gym bag from inside the chest to take his experiment outside.

Once deep enough in the woods where no one could watch, he threw the cord over a sturdy tree branch and proceeded to snap his own neck.

He saw the cuckoo bird at ten o'clock and rummaged through the chest to find the straight razor. Soon, he was on the blood-soaked rug with his throat cut wide open. A few minutes later, he awoke again, on the recliner, and the blood was gone.

The Professor ate all the marijuana in the baggie and got halfway through the tedious book before realizing that, though nauseating, it was not life threatening. He stomped out of the secret room and removed the loaded pistol from his desk. He blew his brains out in front of Billy and Beulah. For half a minute, he watched as Billy cried over his dying body, while Beulah just sat on the couch eating a potato chip, eyes glued to her soap opera (*Screw Beulah*), and then he was back on his recliner once again. When he emerged from the room, the couple were still spooning on the couch, and it was like nothing had ever happened.

He went back to his secret room as the cuckoo clock struck noon. The Professor considered that time may not mean much of anything to him anymore.

What was time to a man who would live forever?

What if he burned down the secret room with him in it?

Oh hell, he was too tired to try that right now. Attempted suicide was utterly exhausting. He put his legs up on the recliner and closed his eyes, just glad to finally see some darkness without any bright lights in it.

Chapter 14

Buddy licked his lips and adjusted his pecker, eyes laser-focused on the backside of Officer Turner.

"Buddy," Ralph whispered in his friend's ear. "Stop staring like that. She's liable to arrest you or something."

Buddy reluctantly turned away to gaze at the crowd.

The gymnasium was lined with rows of fold-out chairs. Every one of them was full and facing a podium with a microphone on it. The murmuring of the crowd grew louder and the big hand of the large clock that looked over the basketball court signaled it was two minutes before seven. Officer Turner stood in the back of the gym next to Pastor Pruitt, Kat's dad, and a man in a suit. About a dozen or so other people were gathered back there, including the self-proclaimed Hope Springs Security Force.

Miss Stoddard sat in the front row with a bearded son on either side. On her right was Bucky Stoddard and to her left was Dickey. Both boys were twenty-something and didn't talk much. They sat with quiet, vacant stares, chewing large tobacco plugs that bloated out their lower lips.

Bucky had a white t-shirt tucked into his jeans, with a pack of cigarettes rolled up in one sleeve and straight black hair pulled back into a ponytail. Dickey had a ponytail too. He wore a pair of khakis and a blue t-shirt with the words *PRAY THE GAY TO STAY!* across the front.

Miss Stoddard sat in the middle of her two boys and looked up at the clock to see it was time to start. After some hard work and grunts, she got her large body off the metal chair and waddled into place behind the podium.

"Testing," she said into the microphone, tapping it with one finger to make sure it was on.

She nodded, raised her arms, and spoke in a low, booming voice. "Alright. Let's get started. Be quiet, and that includes you, Sam!"

Everyone got quiet and all eyes faced Miss Stoddard.

"That's better," she continued. "As president of the Community Watch, I called this meeting to talk about all the child abductions that have been going on. We've had eleven of our precious little ones taken in the last several weeks and we all know where the pedophiles live at. Now, as your leader, I would love to get together a group of boys to go over there, knock on their door, and give those perverts a five-fingered welcome to our community. Miss Officer back there calls that vigilante justice, but if they're not doing nothing to keep our little ones safe, then who will? I say we give them until Thursday to clear out, and if they're still there then we pay them a visit. Before we take a vote on it, does anyone have anything to say?"

In the back row, Billy was pulling on his brother-in-law's arm, unsuccessfully trying to keep him from standing up. The Professor released himself from Billy's grip and marched down the aisle. He waved Miss Stoddard to the side and stood directly behind the podium to address the large crowd.

"Dear ladies and gentlemen. I am in complete agreement with Miss Stoddard and feel that if the police aren't going to do anything about the problem, then you should take it into your own hands. Yup. I think it's a great idea. Thank you."

He waved a hand and moved quickly down the aisle as the Stoddard boys gave him a standing ovation. When the Professor rushed out the double doors of the gym, Billy got up and chased after him.

Miss Stoddard resumed her place behind the podium. "Well, I'm glad to see that all the insane people agree with me. Now, anyone else have something to say? Officer Turner?"

The crowd turned around and watched the officer, Kat's father, and the man in the suit all stride down the aisle together. The man in the suit arrived at the podium first.

"Good evening," the man said. "My name is Greg Dicks and I'm the head of the East Hills Home Owner's Association, where some of you currently reside. We're all here today to address the very serious situation regarding the disappearance of Bobby Krisp, Regina Banks, Seth Mangini—"

"We know their names, Greg," a crowd member stood up and yelled. "We just want to know what you're gonna do about it."

The crowd mumbled in agreement as Katrina's dad took Greg's place behind the podium.

"Hello," he began. "I'm Frank Thompson, park supervisor over at—"

"We all know who you are, Frank!" someone yelled.

"Alright, well you also need to know that the police are doing everything they can to find the molester and we are doing what we can to protect our kids. We now have a curfew in the park, and I even tried hiring the local security force to walk through the community. There's just not a lot else we can do. It's up to the police now."

Miss Stoddard grunted and moved to the podium, motioning Frank away. "Frank, you say the police are doing what they can, but that preacher's place is why we're all so angry. Pastor Pruitt is the one harboring pedophiles while our children go missing. It doesn't take Sherlock Holmes to figure out where the child molesters are. So what is being done about those people? What are the police doing about that?"

The officer remained standing next to the podium and spoke loudly without a microphone. "That is a very valid question, Miss Stoddard. My name is Officer Turner, and I have personally been out to Pastor Pruitt's property. Yes, there are five men staying in three small trailers on his church land, but—"

"What church?" Miss Stoddard interrupted. "Does anybody still go there?"

The crowd giggled, but the preacher in the back of the room did not.

"Like I was saying," the officer continued. "Our detectives went out and investigated these men and they willingly opened up their homes. We took forensic evidence and searched all of the properties. We questioned them and found no reason to suspect the men in any of the disappearances."

"No reason?" Miss Stoddard asked. "They're pedophiles and we have little ones missing, officer."

"Yes, but unless there is some direct evidence pointing them to these specific abductions, there is nothing we can do. I'll continue going out there, and the pastor is keeping an eye on his tenants too." The officer leaned her torso in front of Miss Stoddard to speak directly into the microphone. "Also, if any of you step foot on that property Thursday night, then me and several deputies will arrest you."

"You and what army?" Miss Stoddard bellowed into the microphone. "That's the government for you, folks. Completely incompetent to do the one thing they're supposed to do, which is keep us safe. Instead of fighting the bad guys they can't even find, they wind up arresting us for trying to do their jobs for them. Well, I say it's time to stand up to 'em. We got a right as the Community Watch to make a citizen's arrest, and that's what we aim to do. So let the pretty little officer come too, but we're going to that haven of pedophiles on Thursday night and we ain't leaving until one of them is either in jail or hanging from a tree."

Officer Turner, Greg, and Frank all walked down the aisle to the back of the church and stood next to the preacher. Several people in the crowd began whooping and hollering as Miss Stoddard spoke fire and brimstone. However, many of those present left quietly out the back, not wanting to get involved at all. After a few minutes, only half the crowd remained, but they were all riled up and most of them were armed.

Terrence got into his big black truck in the parking lot of the gymnasium while Katrina and Cris sat in an idling sedan with the lights off. The big truck pulled out of the parking lot and Kat followed a safe distance behind.

Cris's phone rang.

"Hello."

"Cris, it's your daddy," Billy said through the phone. "Have you seen Albert?"

"No," Cris said. "We're following Terrence's truck right now. What's up?"

"Well, he got up and made some stupid speech at the meeting and stormed out. When I went outside, he was gone. I'm on the way to the barn and wanted to make sure he wasn't with you."

"Nope," Cris said, smiling at Kat. "I guess we'll check in with you later. Bye, Dad."

"What's going on?" Kat asked.

"Dad can't find Uncle Albert, but he's probably fine. Before we go to the barn, you wanna stop and park somewhere? I mean, after we're done chasing Terrence and all."

"Sure," Katrina replied with both hands on the wheel. "Graduation is in two nights and my dad said I could stay out as late as I wanted. Do you think we could go somewhere other than my car that night?"

"I could get a room in town, if you wanted to. I mean, if you didn't want to do something like that then maybe we could camp out or something."

"A room sounds nice. Can you do that?"

"Yeah. Are you sure?"

"One hundred percent," Kat grinned. "I'm just sorry I made you wait this long to do it. I know it's weird that I'm still a virgin and all. I mean, other than the hardcore Christian kids, I don't know any other ones my age. Guess I just wanted my first time to be with someone I really cared about. I just wanted it to be special, you know?"

Cris nodded. "So, you care about me then?"

"Of course," Kat said. She shrugged her shoulders. "You're the first real boyfriend I've ever had. I mean, I guess I love you, Cris."

Kat took a hand off the wheel and held his tightly on top of the console between them.

"I know we haven't known each other all that long, but I love you too, you know?" Cris said. "I'll get a good room Thursday night. I promise it'll be special."

"Well, it will finally be over at least. The wait I mean," she said. "I don't know why I think it'll be anything special. It will probably be over before we even know it."

"Not if I can help it," Cris said proudly.

"You know what I mean. I've been building it up for so long and..." Kat leaned up in the seat. "Where is he going?"

Both of them looked ahead as they drove past the turn for Terrence's house.

"He's not going home. That's for sure," Cris said.

They were both nervous and stopped talking altogether as they followed the truck down some dark country roads. They tried to stay far enough behind to not be conspicuous but still keep him in sight. Finally, they passed by Terrence parked in a picnic area beside the lake.

"Was that him?" asked Cris as they continued down the windy, narrow road surrounded by trees.

"Yup," Kat answered. "I'm going up here to park on the side of the road. We'll have to walk back to his truck. Did you bring a flashlight?"

"Check."

The two of them got out of the parked vehicle and walked along the gravel road. By the time their eyes adjusted to the pitch-blackness, they were approaching the picnic area.

"There," Kat whispered. "That's his truck."

"I can barely see it. Where's he at?" Cris whispered back.

Kat put a single finger over her mouth for him to be quiet and they walked in the dark along the line of trees, keeping their eyes open for any sign of Terrence. When they got near the truck, Kat pointed to a shaky beam of light shining through the trees along the lake.

"He's walking along the lake," Kat whispered. "Let's leave our light off for a while. I think I see the trail opening over there. Come on."

She grabbed his hand. They jogged to the tiny trail and entered the forest.

The couple followed the flashlight in the distance as the trail became narrower and narrower, and eventually it seemed that the original trail had ended and they were walking down a newly created one. The ground on this new path was still smoking where the brush had been burnt about a foot or two wide through the wildest parts of the forest. The ground was blacker than the darkness, so they were able to follow it easily. The fire had mysteriously been confined to the trail and there was no sign of any other part of the woods being burned.

They had to walk single-file to fit on the pathway, with Kat in front and Cris close behind. The couple walked for over two hours and couldn't stop to rest if they wanted to since neither wanted to sit down on the smoldering floor of the trail, and the weeds on either side were too tall to see anything but straight ahead. So they kept walking, and sometime in the third hour of their trek, Kat heard the heavy breathing approach from behind. She turned to see a figure in the darkness lumbering toward them. She grabbed Cris by the arm and pulled him into the shoulder-high brush to the right of the trail.

They sat up in the weeds and thorns as the figure awkwardly moved past. Kat ignored the scrapes and cuts and stepped back onto the trail. She flicked on her flashlight to see who had almost run them over.

Up ahead, Katrina could see an old woman from behind lumbering away with her arms outstretched in front of her. The woman turned her head slightly and Kat got a quick look at her face. She immediately flicked off the light. The teenager's whole body stiffened in fear as the figure continued moving quietly away from them in the darkness.

"Who was it?" Cris whispered, picking thorns from his arm and standing behind her on the trail. "Did you get a good look?"

Kat nodded. "I did, but I don't know what that thing was. It looked a little like an old woman, but her face... The way the shadows played with that face, it didn't look like an old woman at all."

"You want to turn around?"

"No," Katrina whispered, taking a deep breath. "No. It was probably just an old woman."

"Yeah, but what is an old woman doing all the way out here?" Cris asked.

"I really don't know, but I'm ready to find out."

They followed the sounds of the woman ahead of them for a while. When they could hear her no more, they just followed the trail, going wherever it took them. They had been on the path for over four hours when they first heard the hissing.

"Did you hear that?" Cris whispered.

"It's a snake," Kat replied.

"Snakes, you mean. That sounds like a lot of hissing, and it's coming from up ahead."

"Buddy was right," Kat said.

"Never thought I'd hear that," Cris replied.

They slowed down and approached a clearing up ahead. The hissing grew louder. The teenagers hid behind a tree and watched.

Terrence stood on one end of the clearing holding a flashlight. Behind him was the old woman standing in place and swaying back and forth in the darkness. The hissing grew even louder, accompanied by the sound of rattlers. The dark floor of the clearing was alive, wriggling and squirming with reptilian life.

The clearing brightened and everything was lit up. The couple could clearly see thousands of rattlesnakes squirming on the clearing floor, leaving only two tight circles for the old woman and Terrence to stand in. Then a little boy—Terrence's son—walked out of the forest and the serpents cleared a pathway for him.

The boy sat on the ground surrounded by snakes, wearing a black cloak and chanting quietly with his eyes closed. The clearing was lit up by a bright yellow light that shone out of the trunk of a large tree directly in front of Terrence. There was a low mumbling noise coming from inside the trunk, and it seemed to mirror the sounds the boy made.

Kat held tightly to Cris's hand as the rattles and hissing grew louder. Terrence turned his head to look at the elderly companion and then at the teenagers. His head twitched and jerked to one side, and Katrina could see the man's glowing yellow eyes staring directly at her.

They stood frozen for a moment as a hissing erupted from Terrence's throat. A forked tongue over a foot in length fell out of his mouth and sharp fangs glistened in the yellow light.

Cris pulled Kat away from the trees and back on the trail. They sprinted, hand in hand, occasionally looking over their shoulder to see if they were being pursued. As they got farther away, the hissing disappeared and the couple stopped to rest.

"Did you see what I saw?" Cris asked.

Both of them were breathing hard and had their hands on their knees.

"Yeah," Kat replied. "Terrence is a snake-man or something."

"Don't you remember what my dad said? That stuff about Apep?"

Kat stood upright and gathered her breath. "So, he's the Serpent God thingy? Well, where is the cult?"

"I don't know. I've never seen anything like that in my life. Does that mean the story is true? There really is this demonic, chaos-loving thing and Terrence is helping it?"

"I thought Terrence was the thing?"

"Something was in that tree too," Cris said, starting down the pathway. "Come on. Let's get back to the barn and talk to Billy."

"I hope he knows how to kill it," Kat said, walking behind him.

"That old woman never turned around in the clearing," Cris said. "When you saw her face earlier, what did it look like?"

"Nothing," Kat said. "Her face was just a dark hole of nothing, but what scared me was the movement. There was something wriggling around in that hole, something round, fat, and segmented, with beady yellow eyes."

"A worm?" Cris asked, picking up the pace.

"Not a worm." Kat shuddered as she walked faster along the still smoking and blackened trail. "Worms don't have fangs, do they?"

Chapter 15

THE PROFESSOR SAT ON the recliner in his private room and waited on Prince to walk through the door. It had taken seven failed rescue attempts, but on the eighth try he had finally sprung the man from the Dalton County Jail.

The other night he attempted to blow his brains out in front of a gymnasium full of townsfolk. However, he found out when Billy got home that what everyone saw was not the Professor putting a bullet in his head, but him giving some speech in support of that Stoddard woman of all things. Albert still didn't know why observers always saw the made-up things that they did and not his demise. The selective memory replacement that occurred every time he was about to die was baffling, but he knew it had to do with the Jenkins spell, and as soon as they took care of this Apep problem, he was going to have a talk with that naughty little boy.

After the gymnasium death, he decided that further experiments could wait and that it was his responsibility to right the wrong of Prince's incarceration and prevent his potential murder conviction. He had the means to rescue the little man, so it was up to him to craft a plan, and it took eight attempts before he was finally successful.

The first three plans were smash and grab attempts, where the Professor just got as far as he could into the place before expiring. He brought a couple of Billy's hand grenades each time and got as far as the cell block on the third attempt, but was unable to locate his friend before getting shot in the legs. They almost cuffed him before he could shove the last grenade in his mouth and pull the pin. He had no idea what illusion the officers had experienced those times instead of seeing his head explode.

After that, Albert realized he had to come up with an actual *Ocean's Eleven*-type plan or they might eventually catch him and put him on suicide watch or something. Then it may take days or weeks before he could kill himself and get back to the room again.

The fourth attempt was for informational purposes only. He put on an old thrift store suit and told the guards he was the inmate's attorney. He got signed in and led through the huge security door. They brought Prince out and the Professor got a general layout of the front of the jail. Then he blew his head off with a guard's gun.

The layout of the front part of the jail was fairly simple. There was a lobby with large steel doors that could only be buzzed open by the officer seated in the tiny room behind bulletproof glass. The visitation was done just inside that steel door in the long hallway on two folding metal chairs. So, the Professor's plan was to sign in, meet with Prince, and take out everyone he could. Then he would buzz the steel doors, drag Prince out the front door, and somehow lead the guards away so his friend could escape back to the barn.

On the fifth and sixth attempts, he shot up the tiny room and hallway, using duct tape to keep the doors opened, and managed to walk Prince outside each time. Before the guards arrived, he broke into the trunk of a random vehicle in the parking lot and dumped Prince in it.

He told him to wait until someone got in the vehicle later and drove away, and then to get out and find his way straight to the barn. However, each time he left him in the trunk and ran toward the onslaught to be killed, he had turned on the news to see the story of a failed escape attempt and some strange story about the escaped convict's lawyer returning the prisoner.

He figured they were searching the vehicles, and somehow in their illusion, he was the person that tipped them off. The Professor was about to just keep trying the idea over and over again, hoping the officers would eventually be incompetent enough to not follow protocol at least once, but he didn't want to go through that sequence of events a bunch of times for nothing. So he thought up another plan—a plan that actually worked.

Billy always kept a police uniform in his bedroom closet. It was his uniform from when he was a cop. Albert hid it under his lab coat and made Prince put on the over-sized uniform on the seventh attempt. He ordered the little man to stay behind and wait until other officers arrived, then take the duct tape off the doors and tell them the inmate escaped with the visitor and send them out. Then he was to go outside, hot-wire the transport van, and drive it through the parking lot while everyone chased the Professor.

The uniform was way too large on that attempt, and they figured it out, but after sewing it to fit a much smaller man than Billy, in the chaos of the moment no one gave Prince a second look on the eighth try. Right before the Professor blew his head off, he saw the van pulling onto the road, and every available officer in the place running away from that road and directly at the crazy man waving a gun. When he woke up on the recliner, the news story was about an escaped inmate that was still at large. One of the guards talked about a mysterious suited man that just vanished into thin air.

It was almost six on Wednesday night when Prince finally knocked on the door.

"Professor?" asked Prince, sticking his tiny head through the cracked door.

"Come on in," the Professor said, rising from the recliner. "Sit down."

Prince was still in his little police uniform, but had rolled up the sleeves and pants legs. He looked around the strange room and pointed at the recliner. "There?"

"No, that's my seat. Just sit on the rug," the Professor said, waving him away from the recliner and sitting down on it. "Were you followed? Tell me what you saw once we left the jail."

Prince sat with his legs crossed on the rug at the opposite end of the monstrous Bigfoot head. He started to speak but caught sight of the floating things on the bookshelves and gulped.

The Professor noticed how nervous his visitor was and smiled. "I'm sorry for the decor. Those things in the jars are all dead. There's no need to be scared."

"And this," Prince said, pointing to the man-ape head attached to the rug.

The Professor sighed. "I believe that you just escaped from jail and an almost certain conviction for murder. You've seen a monster eat your friend and myself. After all you've been through, why are you so frightened by a dead Bigfoot and some heads floating in jars?"

Prince shrugged. "I'm not scared, just curious. I'm still trying to figure out exactly what you are, Professor. I mean, how you survived that Priest and all the strange things you did at that jail. Are you some kind of magician or something?"

The Professor blushed and nodded. "Well, yes, apparently I am a wizard...a very novice one, but still a wizard. I think I only have one spell. It's a death spell that I don't really understand fully. That's how I was able to get shot up and still be alive."

Prince looked at the man, confused. "A death spell? I mean, I saw you come to the jail to visit me and you talked a lot about trusting you and I told you about the layout and everything. The first few times you just got up and walked out, but the last time you brought the uniform and had that crazy plan," Prince giggled and shook his head, "and it worked. It actually worked. I mean, the guards came to the front of the jail and I went outside with them, right in the middle of all of them. They went running after you and I got in the van and left. I guess you just vanished somehow, but I'm not sure exactly. I ditched the van in town and got back to my place. I had to get Lil' Red."

"Lil' Red?"

"My motorcycle. It's purple and maroon, but I call it Lil' Red. Anyway, I came right here and brought the cycle into the barn. Is that the death spell? The vanishing act you put on?"

"Kind of," the Professor said.

He told Prince all about the Jenkins boy taking his mortality and about what happens every time he dies.

When he was done, Albert pointed to the TV. "On the news they talked about a man in a suit that vanished into thin air. They think it was an illusion or something, and I don't think they'll connect it to some ex-educator living in a dilapidated blue barn. Somehow right before I die...or expire...or whatever you want to call it, everyone else sees some illusion that masks my demise. The illusion seems to cover a long period of time, like when I tried to burn down this place with myself inside. The fire burned for a while before I died, and when I woke up in the recliner, Billy said I'd been in my room all day. The illusion of me being in my room must have lasted hours that time. Then there was the incident at the gymnasium where the illusion just covered what I did on stage and nothing prior or after that. I don't really understand all the details yet, except the part about me not dying."

"But technically, you do die," Prince said. "You die each time and are reborn again, right there in the recliner. Is it possible that you only have a certain number of lives to use? Like a cat?"

The Professor rubbed his chin. "You know, I haven't thought of it that way. But if the creature was right and the boy took my ability to die, then there should be no limits on it."

"True," Prince said. "So, he had to remove your mortality for the spell to work. The illusions, your painless death, your rebirth in that chair...all of it seems like one long spell that could only work for someone that couldn't die to begin with."

"That's it!" the Professor said. "A long spell. The whole sequence of events is the spell. The illusions are triggered at some point when I know, maybe intuitively, that I'm about to die. Then at some later point, the anesthetic part of the spell is set off, and when my brain activity is completely dead, the last act is to put me on this goddamned recliner. Yes, that's it! Prince, you're a genius!"

"I don't know about that," Prince said with a grin. "But I guess it makes sense for a spell to set things in motion like that."

"It makes perfect sense. The boy told me he had to cast a spell, and that's it. I'm the one that's going to set those things right. I'm part of his spell, which includes all the chain of events that make up the entire plan. The plan is the spell."

"Yeah," Prince said. "He's using you as a weapon of sorts. That's why you intuitively knew where to find the Priest and knew to go to the playground."

"Maybe. I thought that was intuition. The boy may be telling me things like that and it just feels like intuition."

Prince shrugged. "But maybe those intuitions are part of the boy's spells. Maybe your intuition about where to be and what to do are just as much a part of the overall spell as the illusions and your rebirth and everything. It's all interconnected somehow."

"There are no coincidences," Albert muttered to himself.

"What was that, Professor?"

"It was something the boy said. He said that there were no coincidences, and I'm beginning to think he was right."

The two men sat in silence for a few moments before the Professor clapped his hands together. "So, if I am a wizard, then I need an apprentice. Isn't that how it's usually done?"

Prince eyed him suspiciously. "You mean me? Can I become a wizard too?"

"Do you hear voices in your head?"

"No," Prince said, "but Charlie did. He heard this woman's voice all the time. Her name was Ariel."

"Well," the Professor stood up from the recliner, "you may not be a wizard. But I don't figure that you have to be a wizard to be a wizard's apprentice. If you accept, then I'll promise to share and discuss all the mysteries of wizardry with you as I discover them myself. I'll protect you here in this barn, and you can come and go as you please when it gets safer. They believe you're a murderer and will be hunting you for a while. I'll do what I can to hide you if you'll stay here and be my assistant." He said this, then sighed heavily. "You see, I can't tell Billy these things. I love my brother-in-law, but when he gets drunk he talks too much. If he knew I couldn't die, he might send me back to this recliner every time he's got a case of beer in him, just for a laugh. He's drinking way too much to be reliable."

"You want me to be your friend?" asked Prince. "You risked your life to go after that creature with us. Not only that, but you came back for me when you didn't have to. You rescued me. Of course I'll be your apprentice, or whatever it is you want to call it. Professor, I'll always be indebted to you for what you did today, and I'll always be your friend."

The man in the lab coat wiped away a tear and tapped the Bigfoot head with his foot. "Billy is the only friend I've had since Rachel died. If he hadn't found her that way..."

"Found who?" asked Prince.

"My sister." Albert sighed. "About six months after the wedding, a year or so after Cris was born, Billy found her body in the woods not too far from here. She was seated against a tree, and I know he'll never forget how she looked with her skull cut apart like that. Her head like a soup bowl, opened up and half empty. There was...there was a large stick with several prongs on it, like a wood fork, stuck into what was left of her brain. Billy got the cops involved, but he knew it wasn't a human that did that. The footprints around the body were too large, and Billy was a hunter; he saw too many signs that couldn't be explained. So, the detectives went searching for Hannibal Lector, but Billy went hunting the monster...and he found him eventually."

He tapped the huge open mouth of the beast head again. "We didn't really get along too well until then. After we got this creature, we wanted to kill them all. Figured if people out there saw a monster, they could tell us about it and we wouldn't have to go blindly hunting for them. But people never really saw what they thought they saw, and Billy got to drinking, and here we are."

Prince stood up and wrapped his arms around the man and Albert patted him on the back. The embrace was interrupted by a knock at the door.

"Who is it?" asked the Professor.

"Who the shit you think it is?" answered Billy from the other side of the door. "Come on outside! Kat has a story to tell us. Albert, did you get a motorcycle?"

"Yes," he answered. "I'll be right out."

The Professor whispered to his apprentice. "I'll only be a little bit. Just stay in here. Please don't touch the head jars."

Prince nodded and the Professor left, locking the door behind him.

Kat and Cris were seated on the couch next to Billy.

"Hello, Katrina," the Professor said.

The teenager nodded and looked at Billy.

"Um, Albert," Billy said. "They saw something...something paranormal or out of this world or whatever. They're a little freaked out. I tried telling them about the things I've seen, but it only scared them more."

Kat looked up nervously at the Professor. "It was Terrence, but it wasn't him. Billy was telling us about this Apep thing and..."

Cris put his skinny arm around her and spoke. "He was a snake-man, Professor. I mean, he had fangs and a snake tongue and everything. How is that possible?"

"And what are we supposed to do when we come across something like that again?" asked Kat.

"Kill it," the Professor said. "You are supposed to kill an evil thing like that."

"Why?" asked Cris. "I mean, just because someone paid you a few hundred bucks to find a boy or a dog, that doesn't mean you have to fight monsters."

"I wouldn't be killing something like that for the money," Albert said. "If the evil god of chaos, AKA Apep, is actually loose, then someone has to kill it if we don't want to live in a world ruled by the thing...and I, for one, do not."

"But isn't that for the police to do?" asked Kat. "Or maybe Batman?"

"Listen," Billy interjected. "What I think Albert's trying to say is that we're going to get that little girl's brother back. We're going to do this because that boy needs to be saved and it's the right thing to do, and also because she paid us to since the cops won't help her. If you'll recall, Terrence did something to the cops. I don't know what exactly, but he convinced them not to investigate somehow. Cris, if you walked into the police station downtown and told them about something called Apep, they wouldn't believe you. If you insisted and bothered them enough, you might find yourself in a nuthouse. You see, only people that believe in crazy shit like this can do anything about it."

"Alright," Kat said. "Let's say we can take the boy and get him without killing this demon thing. Will that be good enough?"

"Good enough for some," Billy said. "But I think my esteemed brother-in-law is saying it might not be good enough for him. He aims to kill that demon and I do too, but you kids don't have to help. Hell, I don't even know what we're doing sending you out to spy on a snake-man to begin with. It's too dangerous. Why don't you both get out of here and just let me and Albert handle this."

"No," Cris said firmly. "No, I want to help you, Dad. I can't let you go out there by yourself and get killed. If I can help, I will."

"Well, if you're going, then I guess I gotta protect you," Kat said, rolling her eyes. "You are my boyfriend, after all."

Billy grinned at her. "Well, then it's settled. Since I'm an idiot, Cris has to be one. And since he's an idiot, Kat's got to be one too. We've got us an actual monster to kill. This is exciting."

"And I'm an idiot too, I guess," the Professor mused. "Well, since we're all good and stupid now, how do we kill this snake-man?"

"And when do we do it?" asked Kat.

"Tomorrow," boomed a voice from the hallway.

Everyone turned to see Daisy standing in the hall. She was splattered with dried gore and held a recently bloodstained hatchet.

"I just came from following Terrence," she said, walking over to the couch. "I killed about a dozen gigantic rattlesnakes trying to sneak around the side of his place. I saw some police officers parked out front too. When they went in the house, one of them turned their head and their face was just darkness, pitch-black, and there was something wriggling in it that looked like a worm with sharp teeth. Then a bunch of snakes attacked and chased me back to the car. I killed some of 'em, but a couple got their fangs in. You still got that rattlesnake anti-venom I used last year?"

"In the bathroom," Billy said, getting up from the couch. "I'll get it for you."

"Thanks," Daisy said. "So, before I got bit, I heard the officers talking to each other as they got in their cars. They were talking about being at a place called Hells Bells tomorrow night."

"Hells Bells!" exclaimed the Professor. "That's it! That's when it's all happening."

"What are Hells Bells, Professor?" asked Kat.

"Whenever a major demon is summoned, it is said that the summoning is sometimes accompanied by the sounds of bells tolling, bells that clang atop the churches of Hell."

"There are churches in Hell?" asked Cris.

"Of course," the Professor said.

"So, let me get this straight." Daisy leaned against the couch. "They're talking about meeting at some place to summon a demon from Hell?"

"Not Hell like you're thinking," Billy said, returning and handing the syringe to Daisy. "That's the story, the metaphor from the Bible. Who knows where the demon actually comes from, and where the bells are actually ringing. Like most myths, until you see it for yourself, you don't know if it's really true or not. Either way, it doesn't really matter where this demon serpent is from. It's more important that we know they are going to meet in a clearing in the woods to try and summon it."

"At least we know what clearing they're talking about." Cris sighed. "It's not technically cleared, with all the snakes wriggling around in it, but I think it's the one."

"Exactly!" the Professor said. "So we just go to that trail by the lake tomorrow night, follow it down to the clearing, and get the boy. Then we kill Terrence the snake-man and prevent the summoning of the chaos demon."

Daisy shook her head as she pulled the needle out of her arm and applied pressure. "Say what?"

"Daisy, you like killing things, right?" asked Cris.

"Yes."

"You want to kill some more snakes and possibly some of those worm-faced things?" asked Kat.

Daisy grinned and nodded. "You mean I get to take out some worm-faced cops?"

"If they aren't human, then I don't care what they're wearing, you can chop their heads off," Billy said.

"Count me in," Daisy said. "Tonight was the most excitement I've ever had around here. What time tomorrow night?"

"Get here just before dark," the Professor said.

"What exactly are they summoning up again?" Daisy asked.

"It's called the demon of chaos," Billy began. "The stories are that when it comes, it wipes out whole civilizations. It usually takes the form of a great serpent and carries with it a plague of madness. This madness can create an insane bloodlust in the living things it infects, and you can imagine how a world full of infected, blood-lusting people can end pretty quickly. It also attracts all of its followers, which means inhuman ones too. Monsters from all over the world might be coming out of the woodwork. It's said that when Apep appears, the dead will rise and monstrous things will come out of the shadows to join their Dark Lord."

"Cool," Daisy said.

"Yeah, and all those snakes and worms in people's faces, those aren't just cute little creatures," the Professor said. "Each and every one of them is some kind of demonic acolyte of the deity themselves. They are the followers of Apep in that other world, Hell or whatever you want to call it. They may have taken the form of snakes and worms, but I bet that's not their original form. Most likely, a sorcerer would have had to bring them here. It could be Terrence that got took over and is doing it, or it could be that cloaked child you saw in the woods, the child we're supposed to find. He may have been a very naughty boy indeed. We'll need to keep his mouth shut if he is the wizard, that's for sure."

"What about the Boogeyman?" asked Kat.

The Professor snapped his fingers. "That's right! Dolly mentioned the Boogeyman that came into their room that night. So, either the Boogeyman is behind it all and not the naughty boy, or they both are. Whoever it is, they have to be the ones that summoned the minions, like the one in Terrence's body, in the first place."

"If a person is magically summoning the demon, then if we shut him up it will all just stop, right?" asked Cris.

"The things that are already here are connected to the thing in Terrence somehow, since he seems to be their leader," Billy said. "We need to stop whoever is behind all this from ever summoning Apep, and then we probably need to cut Terrence's head off."

"Sounds like a plan," Daisy said, raising her bloody hatchet.

"And my money's on the kid being behind it. Albert has already seen one pre-pubescent wizard recently," Billy said, downing the rest of his beer.

"Professor," Cris began, "what if they're successful? What if that demon-thing is summoned into this world? Will it take a human host like the other things did?"

"No," Albert said. "Billy can correct me if I'm wrong, but it's my understanding that when Apep itself is brought forth, it is usually in the form the Master chooses. Something like that doesn't need a host in this world like the minions do."

Billy nodded. "That's right. So, to answer your question, son, if it is summoned then not even a thousand Daisys armed with tanks and machine guns would be able to kill something that powerful. Demons like that fight battles in our minds, battles they almost always win."

"So if it gets here, then we should all just go to an island somewhere and wait for the world to burn? Is that what you're telling me?" asked Cris.

"Yes," the Professor said. "That is precisely what we are saying."

Part Three:
Graduation

Chapter 16

A TALL, THICK WOMAN in a pantsuit stood behind the podium on a small stage at one end of the high school gymnasium. Behind her, a short man in a suit stood next to a table full of diplomas. The bleachers on both sides were only half-filled with friends and family. All the graduates were seated in their metal chairs beside the stage, quietly listening to Principal Bonita, nicknamed Principal Boneshaker by the students.

"Now, we are gonna call everyone up one by one. Please just clap respectfully when the name is called. Don't whoop and holler or the next graduate's family won't get to hear their precious one's name. Also, let's clap a little bit for everybody, not just your graduate. We should be proud of all of them, whether they got family or not. Got it? Good." She paused and cleared her throat. "Brandon Aken."

There was a spatter of polite applause. The boy got his diploma from the assistant principal in the suit and walked off the other side of the stage. The remaining teens were standing now, waiting for their names to be called.

"Stephanie Baker."

Some applause, followed by a whoop that quickly ceased with one glance from the Boneshaker.

"Robert Bingham."

Katrina knew it would take a while to get to the T's. She smiled at Cris, who nervously waved back at her. She was finally graduating, but considering what had happened lately it just didn't seem quite as important anymore. Katrina had been concerned about her future after high school and saying goodbye to a place that she really wasn't going to miss all that much anyway...but now, all she could think about was how to kill a snake-man.

The girl's adrenaline was pumping. She was ready to hurry up and get that diploma so her and Cris could have another adventure together. He was so brave, volunteering to help Billy like that. She would have never guessed he would willingly go back to that clearing again to kill monsters. It was a side of her boyfriend that Kat had not seen before, and she had never wanted to get to a hotel room so badly in her life.

Unfortunately, they would have to wait one more night. Cris moved the reservation to Friday, so they now had something to look forward to if they survived the evening. Which brought her mind back to the original nagging question.

How do you kill a snake-man?

"Delores Goodman."

Kat's cell phone vibrated and she took it out to see a message from Cris.

GOT TXT FROM DAISY. EMERGENCY! GOT TO LEAVE B4 IT ENDS. SORRY. GO TO BARN AS PLANNED. SEE YOU AT TRAIL. LOVE U.

She read it and looked up to see Cris nervously waving again. She smiled and waved back. Katrina had considered having a talk with him about saying *I love you* so much, but she just couldn't bring herself to do it. She liked it sometimes, and figured if she brought it up then he would probably never say it to her the same way ever again.

"Lauren Locke."

Cris waited anxiously in the bleachers to clap louder than anyone else had clapped before when his girlfriend's name was called. He was excited for her and didn't want to leave early, but Daisy said it was important. Her exact message was pretty urgent.

GET TO TRAIL NOW! EMERGENCY!

Cris had also got a message from his dad.

DAISY IS IN TROUBLE. WE'RE OLD AND YOU'RE CLOSER. GO TO HER AND WE WILL WAIT FOR YOUR WIFE TO GET DONE WITH GRADUATION.

This was followed by a crude emoji of a finger going in and out of a fist.

"Jimbo Mooney."

Cris looked over and saw Katrina's mom getting her phone ready to take a picture, her dad smiling like the happiest man on earth, and her little stone-faced brother in a t-shirt that said something in cursive French.

"Hey there, skinny," said a giggling voice with a heavy Southern drawl, seated somewhere behind Cris.

He half-turned to see a girl who looked barely old enough to drive smiling seductively at him next to her naughty-looking friend. They had giggled the whole ceremony, and he had tried to ignore them all night. The girl touched his shoulder and Cris swatted it away.

"Stop that," he said a little too loudly. "Don't touch me."

There were several shushes and Kat's parents looked in his direction for a moment.

"Yolanda Price."

"I like you," the girl whispered in his ear through her giggles. "You look like a sexy scarecrow."

Cris stayed calm and, without turning around, he whispered out the side of his mouth, "Where is your mother?"

"She's gotta work tonight," the girl whispered back. "You wanna come home with me?"

Cris swatted her hand away again. "No."

"Randall Stinson."

Cris was not looking forward to going down that trail again, but he knew that Kat wanted to and he couldn't let her down. They had talked about getting an apartment in town and moving in together in the fall. He'd never had an actual girlfriend before and had never loved anyone like he loved Kat. Cris was as happy as could be and couldn't stop thinking about Friday night.

He bought some rose petals and dozens of tiny candles to decorate the room with, and had been masturbating like crazy so he could last longer. He had bought about a dozen condoms and some lubricant that smelled kind of nice. Cris wanted it all to be perfect, a perfect night that both of them would remember when they were sitting on their front porch for their fiftieth wedding anniversary. His dad had told him not to rush things or he might scare her off, but she seemed to love him as much as he loved her. Besides, he wasn't planning on buying a ring or anything for at least another month.

His phone buzzed and he looked at the message from Kat.

LOVEU2

Cris's eyes welled up a little. He slapped the tiny hand from his shoulder two more times and then...

"Katrina Thompson."

Cris stood up and clapped, and so did the two little girls behind him. Between them and Katrina's family, it was the loudest applause of the night.

Chapter 17

"So you're gonna protect us, right?" asked a short, beady-eyed man in his forties. "That Stoddard lady wants blood this time."

"We'll protect you, Stanley," replied Officer Turner. "We will have somebody out here at all times."

Stanley stood nodding his head next to three other men of various ages and builds. All of them would be homeless if not for the benevolence of Pastor Pruitt, and all of them were registered sex offenders.

"I can't thank you enough, Officer," the preacher said in tight jeans and a polo shirt. "It's just ungodly how the town is treating these poor men."

Officer Turner caught Stanley looking at her chest and sighed uncomfortably. "Well, I guess. Just don't worry about the Stoddards. We'll keep somebody—"

"Mommy!" yelled a cute little eight-year-old boy who was running from the cop car.

All the men, except for the pastor, squirmed and avoided looking at the child as he ran full-speed toward them.

"Get your ass back in that car, Winston!" Officer Turner yelled. "Go on."

The boy stopped dead in his tracks and ran back to the vehicle as fast as he had come.

"Alright then, I guess I'll see you later," the officer said. "I've got to get Winston home for now, but I'll be right back. Officers Cranston and Higgs are in the pastor's trailer and they should be enough to fend off any pending posse while I'm gone. Pastor, can I speak with you alone for a minute?"

She led the preacher away from the nervous sex offenders. When they got to the police car, the roar of HEMI engines and country music erupted from down the road.

Ten large trucks loaded with people lined up along the side of the street. They blocked the driveway and revved their loud engines.

Officers Cranston and Higgs came out of the pastor's place with hands on holstered weapons, while the four grown men ran full-speed past them into the mobile home. The three officers stood in the pastor's yard and eyed the loud gang of vigilante trucks. A passenger door opened on a monstrous vehicle, with wheels taller than most adults, and Miss Stoddard stepped gingerly down the stairs.

"Shut that shit off!" she yelled above the twanging guitars and deep, rumbling trucks.

One by one, all the engine-roaring and catchy tunes ceased. The setting sun was bright behind the truck that blocked the driveway.

It was a monstrous vehicle with the two Stoddard boys standing in the bed wearing full camouflage. The Mastiff named Bitch growled through the open passenger-side window. The matriarch of the family waddled over to the police officers, breathing heavy in plus-size hunting gear.

"Hello there, Preacher," she said.

"You've put on your show," said Officer Turner. "Now get out of here before we arrest you."

"Or shoot you," said the younger of the two male deputies standing behind her.

"Alright. Let's just hold on now," Officer Turner said. "There ain't gonna be any shooting today. Right, Miss Stoddard?"

"Officer, please. We just come to welcome the four gentlemen peeking through that window over there." The large woman grinned and gave a friendly wave. "Hey there, gentlemen!"

"Is that it?" asked the pastor.

"Hell no, that ain't it!" yelled the Stoddard boy wearing a pink bandana and holding a shotgun. "We're gonna wait until you leave and then we'll really give 'em a warm welcoming. Cops can't stay here forever, and you'll never know which one of us did what since you wasn't here. Vigilante justice is what I'm taking about!"

"Shut up, boy!" Miss Stoddard yelled back. "You just shut your goddamn mouth! You hear me? Lord, that child's caused me nothing but heartache, but he's still my baby. Those missing children were someone's baby once too, and those devils peering out that window over there took 'em. It's like a window into Hell, and you call yourself a preacher. You should be ashamed, Jimmy Pruitt!"

"That boy of yours ain't no child," said one of the deputies. "That's Harry Stoddard. He graduated with me."

"Sure is," agreed Officer Turner. "Harry's old enough to know better than to be holding that shotgun. If I'm not mistaken, that boy of yours is on probation. I think trespassing and illegal possession of a firearm should put him back in county."

"What gun?" the woman grunted and turned around. "Harry! Put that damned weapon down right now." She turned back to the officers as the boy laid down the gun in the bed of the truck. "My boy ain't holding no gun, and he ain't trespassing neither. That's a public road we're parked on."

Suddenly, a truck with the word SECURITY on it pulled off the road and parked itself in the front yard. Buddy and Ralph got out and rushed to join the negotiation.

"Evening," Ralph said, tipping his SECURITY hat and yanking up his Wranglers by the belt buckle.

"Hey, Ralph," said one of the deputies. "Buddy."

Officer Turner blew out a frustrated breath and turned on the two members of the Security team in matching hats. "Get in your goddamned truck and get out of here. Now!"

Buddy stopped and put his hands on his hips. He was wearing a tight white t-shirt and gym shorts. "Nice to see you too, Officer Turner. We ain't harming nobody and we're just here to help you out, that's all." He turned to the crowd of vehicles and put his hands up. "Everyone just go home now, alright. These men got rights, just like you do."

Officer Turner stepped closer to the posse's large leader and whispered into Miss Stoddard's ear. "I'll tell you what. You get that group out of here and I'll see what I can do about Jerry's application. He applied for the force, didn't he?"

"Yeah, but what can you do?" Miss Stoddard asked.

"I can put a good word in. Hell, he can have my goddamned job if he wants it. Just get these people out of here. I'm tired and got my own boy in the car who I don't want in the middle of all this bullshit."

"Hmmm," the woman opined. "Jerry could use the work. Harry's always up to no good on that weed and all, but Jerry's different."

"I can pull his application. As long as he don't muck up the interview or fail some drug test, then he should get hired. Hurry up though, that offer won't stand for long," Turner said, glaring at the other woman.

Suddenly, there was a loud hissing noise from the woods behind the trailers. Everyone's eyes watched the floor of the forest slither back and forth and a sea of serpents flooded out of the trees. Thousands of reptiles surrounded the trailer and all the people present...and no one tried to run. They all just stood perfectly still.

The four men in the trailer watched through the window as the serpents retreated back into the woods, and all the people followed behind them. It was like the snakes were showing them the way or something. As the serpents passed by the trailer window, all the sex offenders shrieked and turned away in horror...all except for Stanley.

He kept watching as the people lumbered by clumsily, almost sleepwalking into the woods. He saw Miss Stoddard waddle past the window. The woman turned her head in his direction, but she didn't have a face. Where there should be a mouth, chin, nose, and eyes, there was only darkness. Then, as he looked closer, something moved.

"Over here," Daisy said in a hushed voice, waving her hand in the dark. "I'm over here."

It was pitch-black as Cris approached her at the picnic table.

"Hey, I got your text," Cris began. "I called on the way here, but you didn't answer. What's wrong?"

"There's no service," Daisy said. "I mean, there was on the way in, but once I got parked and out of the car, I couldn't get any signal. Terrence left his house early and there was a line of cars following him. Did you see all the cars parked on the side of the road when you came in?"

"Yeah. They're all here with Terrence?"

Daisy nodded. "I followed them and parked down the road. I watched a line of twenty or thirty people walking like zombies into that trail over there. It was still light then so I could see clearly, and the ones I saw had worm faces. I didn't want to shoot them just yet. I kind of wanted someone else here with me before I started killing the things."

"They're not things. They're still people, just possessed people or something. Should we go ahead and follow them?" asked Cris.

Daisy shrugged. "I think we should. Everyone else can catch up later. I brought some artillery for you."

She turned on her flashlight and pointed it at the picnic table. There was a samurai sword, something that looked like an Uzi, and a handgun.

"I'll take this, I guess." He shrugged and grabbed the handgun.

"Here," Daisy said, sticking a small hatchet down his belt loop. "Wear this in case we need to cut something's head off. It's real sharp and I've got two of them."

She picked up the automatic weapon and the samurai sword. Cris could see her more clearly with the flashlight on. Her muscles, and breasts, bulged out of the short-sleeved t-shirt. She held the automatic rifle and had a handgun on one hip, a hatchet on the other, a baseball bat strapped over her back, and the samurai sword dangling from her belt.

"Let's go," Daisy said, and led Cris down the trail.

It only took a few minutes before they could hear the hissing from somewhere far away. As they walked down the dark path, Cris checked his phone for messages and saw that there wasn't any service. He pulled up the message screen and read off the last few exchanges he'd had with Kat on the way there.

LEAVING NOW. TRYING 2 GET OUT OF HERE. JUST GLAD ITS OVER. HEADING TO BARN.

ALMOST TO DAISY. CONGRATS AGAIN! LOVE U!

LUVU2

Cris kept walking as the trail narrowed and they started on the tight blackened path that had been smoking when he and Kat had walked it the other night. He followed Daisy in single file and couldn't help but smile.

LUVU2

Kat didn't say things like that very often. They might not have known each other that long, but Cris didn't care. He had always been a romantic at heart, and dreamed of getting married and living in the suburbs with four or five kids. He knew it was old fashioned and boring for someone his age to want that stuff, but he truly believed that everyone had that one special person out there that they were meant to find. Whether Kat realized it or not, he just knew they were soulmates.

About an hour down the trail, the hissing grew much louder. Daisy stopped and removed the hatchet from her belt. She swung the weapon down on the ground like a barbarian and came up holding the top half of a dying, wriggling, worm-like body of what had been a huge serpent.

"Got one," she whispered. "Look."

Daisy pointed behind them on the trail to some movement in the darkness from where they had come.

"Are those snakes?" whispered Cris.

"I don't know. Come on. Let's keep moving."

Cris followed Daisy down the path. A little snake crawled past him, and then another. Then a large one came out of the woods to his left. It slithered over his foot, causing him to stop dead in his tracks as it went forward past Daisy and three others rushed by. Daisy stopped up ahead and motioned to the left.

"Get off the trail!" she said in a loud whisper and jumped into the woods to the left of the path.

Cris turned to see a mass of slithering things moving in the darkness and approaching fast. The mass was almost as tall as him. He gulped, steadied himself, and fell into the weeds and branches to the left.

"Ouch," he said, crawling through a thorn bush.

Cris found a tree and lay down on the ground with his back to it. He looked around in the dark, but was unable to see Daisy, the path, or even any snakes. The hissing was deafening though, and he figured Daisy couldn't call out to him until it quieted down.

He saw movement in his line of vision and squinted. In front of him, through the weeds and brush, Cris saw something on all fours coming his way. He figured it was Daisy, but then it got closer. As it approached, he saw the fish-faced thing's huge eyes, and oval-shaped lips. Then he felt the scaly hand cover his mouth as the ground rushed beneath him.

He was flying over the earth, through the wildest parts of the forest. His abductor shattered tree branches and made a trail of its own through the woods. The teenager's feet bounced off the forest floor as he was dragged along so fast that the hissing noises faded away in a matter of seconds. He heard only the trilling sound of the monster holding him as the forest rushed past and the scaly grip on his face tightened. The smell of mud and ancient water filled his nostrils.

He was dragged out of the forest and saw the shores of the lake move past him. His eyes widened and he screamed into the reptilian hand. As the water hit his legs, he gasped one last time before being pulled below the surface. Once fully submerged, Cris was moving even faster than before, down into the depths of the lake.

The thing carried him deeper and deeper into the darkest parts of Lake Warren. Just as his head felt like it was going to explode with pressure, the hand opened up for a moment and he inhaled reflexively, choking on the dirty liquid. The scaly hand went back over the mouth as the water filled his lungs, and then filled his entire body. The blackness became even darker, and Cris felt a pop inside of his skull just before his body seemed to float away from him.

Chapter 18

KATRINA CAME TO A stop at the red light and picked up her cell phone.

ALMOST TO DAISY. CONGRATS AGAIN! LOVE YOU! LUVU2

She was running late. Kat was in the same black t-shirt and shorts she had worn under her graduation robes. After taking pictures with her parents and her science teacher Ms. Timmons, Amy Plowman stopped her and babbled on and on for ten minutes about how sad it all was. By the time Katrina left school, it had taken almost an hour and was completely dark outside.

The light turned green and Kat squealed out. She darted from lane to lane in the little sedan. She knew that Cris was already on that spooky trail. She wanted to go down that dark path with him, their adrenaline pumping, facing the unknown together. It had taken her some time to admit it, but Katrina was very much in love with him...dorky little grin and all.

She turned off the highway and into the trailer park, speeding down the gravel road. The place was empty. No one was on their porch or in their yard, and the lights were off in all the mobile homes. They were probably off raiding the preacher's place, but it was still really weird. She had never seen the park that quiet after dark. Katrina pulled up to

Billy's place, parked the car on the side of the road, and ran into the barn.

The lights were off inside and it was completely dark. She fumbled against the wall for a light switch, but couldn't find one. Katrina went back outside and saw a light on in the shed behind Billy's trailer. She jogged toward it and could see the outline of three men standing just outside the tiny building.

"Billy?" the girl asked as she came to a stop behind them.

All three men turned around to face her. The Professor was in his lab coat next to Daisy's boy toy, Will. Billy walked out of the shed holding a half-case of beer.

"Kat," Billy said with a smile. "Congratulations, graduate. Welcome to adulthood."

"Congratulations, Katrina," said Will, flashing perfect teeth.

The Professor nodded to her uncomfortably.

"Thanks," she replied. "We ready to go?"

"Of course," the Professor said. "We were just picking out some weapons."

Billy lifted a hoe in the air. "Got this thing in case I run out of bullets."

Kat saw the firearm on Billy's hip and asked, "Can I get a gun too?"

"You ever shot one before?" asked Billy.

"No."

"Then you don't get one," Billy said. "How about you grab something sharp from in here?"

Katrina could see the tools dangling from the interior walls of the building. There was a large chainsaw, several big hammers, and all sorts of sharp objects. Will grabbed a sledgehammer with a shortened handle off the wall and followed Billy out of the shed. Kat saw the Professor looking nervously at her.

"What's your weapon?" she asked.

"Well, I got my gun," he patted the pistol holstered underneath his lab coat, "and I got my brain," he tapped a finger on his forehead and then crossed his arms, "but I can't figure out which sharp tool to take for killing snakes."

Kat reached forward and grabbed the chainsaw. "How about this?"

His eyes bulged and the Professor snatched the weapon and put it back on the wall. "No chainsaws!"

Katrina shrugged. "Alright. Well, I'll just take the axe."

She grabbed a short-handled hatchet and watched the Professor make his decision.

He looked at the can of gasoline, then a pack of matches, and shook his head. Sighing, he grabbed a long screwdriver.

"Ready?" asked the man in the lab coat.

Katrina nodded and led the group to her car.

"Daisy messaged me when she got there," Billy said, "and Cris messaged about an hour ago. So we can assume they are already down the trail."

"Then we got some catching up to do," Will said, opening the back door. "Let's get going."

The four of them climbed into Katrina's car and she barreled over the gravel and onto the highway. The roads were empty and they didn't pass any cars going out to the lake. When they got close to the entrance, Will rolled down the window and all of them could hear the snake tongues in unison. Scattered vehicles littered the sides of the road. There was one abandoned truck after another, some of them with their engines still idling.

As they got closer to the turn, Kat leaned forward and squinted to see through the misty darkness. The street moved and slithered where the turn was.

"There are hundreds of them!" Will said.

"More like thousands," said Kat. "Hold on!"

The tires squished through the piles of slimy-skinned creatures, with snake guts and blood splattering the exterior of the sedan. The car bounced over the dead reptiles as it turned into the lake entrance.

The street soon cleared of snakes and Kat drove through the maze of abandoned vehicles until they saw Cris's little car on the side of the road. They parked behind it and walked toward the picnic area.

"The trail starts in the clearing up ahead where the tables are," Kat said.

"Who are all these people?" asked Billy as he downed a can of beer and threw it in the woods.

"They've been called out here by something," the Professor said. "They probably all have worm faces too."

"I saw a cop car on the way in," Will said. "There is no telling who's in those woods."

"It doesn't matter who else is in there," Kat said. "Cris and Daisy are there right now. So let's get to them, and then we can figure out a plan."

They reached the picnic area, which was illuminated by the moon and the waters of the lake. In the row of trees on one side, there was a dark hole where the trail began. They could hear serpents all around...thousands of hissing tongues hidden somewhere in the dark forest.

"Daisy and Cris should be up ahead somewhere," the Professor whispered as the four of them paused at the mouth of the trail. "Are you sure there were no turns in there?"

Kat nodded. "I'm sure. It was just one straight shot all the way to the clearing. It took a few hours of walking, but... What's that?"

Katrina pointed behind them to a picnic table with what looked like a person seated and slumped over it. She jogged in the dark and the others followed.

"Is it Cris?" Billy asked.

Katrina reached the table first. The moonlight shone on the slumping figure. It was seated on the bench with the torso resting on the wooden tabletop. The scrunched-up and wrinkled face was turned her way. It was so deflated that it looked like a rubber mask with holes for eyes. The naked, glistening body was so white that it glowed, and the whole sagging mess dripped with water.

Kat extended a hand toward its shoulder and pressed down, but there was nothing underneath the shell and her hand pressed the squishy thing all the way down to the wood. She almost fell over, barely catching herself on the table with the other hand, before quickly pulling away.

"It's empty," she whispered to herself, suddenly noticing the ripped opening down the back where the spine had been. The entire thing was nothing more than an empty bag of pale skin.

"Cris?" asked Billy, stepping up behind Kat and leaning down to get a closer look at the face. It was wrinkly and lifeless, with two empty eye holes, but the features somewhat resembled his son. He bent down and slowly stroked the skin bag's crinkled head.

Kat was crying, but she refused to believe that the deflated husk of skin slumped over the table was Cris. She just knew he was still alive, and while Billy was stroking the empty vessel, she wiped the tears and closed her eyes. Katrina tried to remember the goofy face smiling from the bleachers just a few hours earlier. When she opened them, all three men stared at her.

"It's not Cris," she told them through gritted teeth. "I'm not sure what it is or what it means, but Cris is still alive and out here somewhere. I can feel it. I just know he's not dead."

"We'll find him," Billy said, resting a hand on her shoulder.

Kat strode past Billy.

"I'm taking the thing with me," she said, more to herself than anyone else.

She folded the empty skin bag four times, pressed it dry against the table, and then tucked it underneath her arm like a plastic tarp.

The Professor approached Billy and whispered, "Don't you think you and her should go back to the barn? That girl is obviously in shock, and you just found your son's empty skin bag, for God's sake."

"You don't know it's him," he responded, icily glaring at his brother-in-law. "There is some strange shit happening at this lake and I'm going to find my boy. If he's alive, then Cris is down that path. So that's where I'm going."

Kat walked past both men and entered the trail.

"Hell, Billy," the Professor began. "You saw that face—"

"Albert!" Billy growled through clenched teeth, still clutching what remained of his half case of beer. "I realize he may be dead. I don't need you to tell me that. But I won't ever know what happened to him if we just stand here jacking off."

Billy wiped his eyes and followed Katrina down the dark path in the trees.

"Did you see the way it folded up?" Will whispered, absently staring at the lake. "How is that possible?"

"I don't know," the Professor said, standing next to Will and watching the moonlit water. He put his arm around the boy toy. "Lots of impossible things seem to be happening lately. Come on. Let's see what's in those woods."

Chapter 19

CRIS AWOKE ON A gurney made of algae at the bottom of the lake. The gurney appeared to have been formed out of the wet earth beneath him. He looked down to see his naked body held in place by three hulking, fish-faced creatures. One held his feet, one held the right arm, and the other the left. They had large, flappy gills and their bodies were covered with hard, blue-green scales. The hands were webbed and huge with sharp claws at the end. They were tall as a basketball goal and hairless, with gaping mouths and glassy eyes aimed right at him.

To his right, he saw five of the creatures in bright green robes. Each one sat cross-legged in front of their own tiny fire. Their mouths were moving but Cris couldn't hear what they said. He tried to speak, but his mouth was full of water...and he suddenly realized his whole body was full of water too.

Why wasn't I drowning?

How did they have fire underwater?

A towering monster, a whole foot taller than the others, came into view and floated toward him through the water. He did not panic. The thing stroked his brow and Cris did not resist. He knew this female loved him.

Maybe it was all a dream?

The three creatures let go of his body and floated away, stopping beside their robed friends. He still couldn't move, no matter how much he tried. The female that loved him cupped what looked like three green eggs in one hand, and with the other she pointed one sharp claw over his stomach and slit him from belly button to sternum.

He felt no pain and watched as the hole widened and the female placed the green eggs inside. Then she gently stroked along the opening and it closed itself back up, the skin forming together as if there had been no cut at all.

Was it a dream?

The earth rumbled beneath him and an ancient thing roared from far away. The female grinned, showing a row of sharp needles, and then placed her lips over Cris's mouth. He felt the heat emanating from the creature as some type of liquid flowed from her into him. Cris gazed into those glassy fish eyes and felt the eggs burning within his belly as the succulent juices flowed throughout his vessel.

His sight went blurry, then came into focus to see another female now seated in a high-backed throne where the little fires and the robed creatures had been before.

She was their master, their leader...their queen.

He heard a trilling noise in his head and somehow knew what it meant. The trill narrated a story of a great scaly witch beneath the sea, who birthed a civilization and named this woman their queen. There were other stories and images of much older, long-extinct civilizations. He felt close to these creatures, and for some reason he was not scared.

The queen watched him with glassy eyes and spoke noiselessly into the water. Everything shook and shivered all around him. He blinked and the queen was gone, and he was floating next to the female with the needle teeth that had kissed him on the gurney. All around them were little fires of different colors with groups of the scaly creatures seated cross-legged behind them. They watched him float past and he realized that his belly no longer burned.

There was a fish-faced child seated with her parents at one of the blue flames.

There was a single, pink-skinned male seated at a white flame.

There were tiny lights far away in the distance and tiny fires of different colors beyond that. It seemed there was no end in sight.

It was a whole new world beneath the lake he had lived beside all his life. The ground shook beneath him again, and bubbles formed and floated past his body. There was something under the lake floor, something powerful and ancient that the creatures feared.

Cris blinked again and the water was racing past. The female's scaly hand held his tiny, delicate fingers as they sped through the water together. His ears popped and his brain squeezed as the waters rushed past. He didn't think to look at his body, but if he had, Cris would have seen that his nude vessel was ghostly pale and shining in the dark water.

Then he blinked a third time, and he was seated at a picnic table. He was naked and his stomach burned again. Cris fell onto the table and writhed in agony, but he couldn't force a scream. It hurt too much to make a sound.

It wasn't just his belly either. Every inch of his skin burned and he wanted to rip the flesh apart just to put out the flames. He was soaking wet, his hands clammy, but his insides were on fire. He reached behind and clawed at his spine. Somehow, he got a little hole ripped in the paper-thin flesh, and then made the hole bigger and bigger until the husk just fell away. Cris shed the skin of his former body and stepped away from the table. He saw that there was no blood and realized that the burning had stopped.

He felt refreshed and full of energy, his body tingling. Cris wanted to see what he was now, so he lumbered to the lake and tried to find his reflection in the moonlit surface. He stared into the water and saw two glassy, lidless eyes staring back at him. He reached up to feel the blue-green scales around his gaping, open mouth, and he wasn't sad. It was as if he had always been that way and was just now seeing his true self for the first time. There were vague memories of a former life, a life as another creature, but those memories were slowly disappearing and slipping away like his flesh.

Cris heard a car door close and slid effortlessly into the water. Floating with his head just above the surface, he heard the whispers from the picnic tables and saw the group of humans. It was dark, but he could see as if there was light everywhere...a green light that permeated everything. There was the Professor, Will, his dad, and a girl he had loved. He remembered the girl's name—Kat—but struggled to recall the memories of time spent together.

A chair by the lake...he remembered that.

There was the feel of her lips on his, but the memories were fleeting. He watched the group as they studied the skin suit and saw the girl wipe her eyes, then all of them disappeared into the forest.

There was a trilling sound and he turned to see the female that loved him, the one that had planted the green eggs inside his belly. He trilled back and then snatched a floating snake and bit its head clean through with his needle-sharp teeth. The serpent tasted good and he nodded to his new family. The female nodded back and then raced through the water, and Cris followed.

Moving swiftly through the lake, he began to recall a bit more of his life before the gurney under the lake.

His name had been Cris and he loved a girl named Kat.

He knew that she was in danger, and no matter what, he had to protect the things he loved.

The two of them swam to the shore and stood side by side, dripping water on the rocks. Cris saw the female next to him and realized that they both must be very tall. He felt strong and could feel his new muscles bulging as they ran through the forest and arrived at the mouth of a cave.

He followed his companion into the rock and saw a bald-headed boy seated cross-legged behind a small fire. A huge black knight stood behind him with arms crossed.

"Not another one, Maggie," the boy said, sighing and waving for the female to come sit beside him. "Come here, my child."

She sat beside the boy and Cris remained standing. The boy shook his head in disgust.

"Maggie, you promised me you would stop procreating. I told you to set up the queen and leave that civilization alone. We're leaving to-morrow, and here you are still transforming people." The boy turned to Cris. "Can you trill yet?"

Cris trilled something that he meant to be his name and the boy looked shocked.

"Maggie, did you take that gawky kid from the park? He was sup-posed to help that new wizard out later tonight." The female bowed her head and the boy threw his hands up. "Oh well. The spell weaves what the spell weaves. Cris, what do you remember?"

Cris trilled about the girl he loved being in trouble, and told the boy all that had happened to him since the gurney.

When Cris finished, the boy nodded. "Maggie, take him to the tree and let him help his girlfriend. She must be worried sick about him."

The female trilled something and the boy put a hand on her shoul-der. "I know. You don't want to harm anyone, but you may have to. Apep will be calling for you and you must be strong. Also, the cloaked wizard behind all of this and the creature inside Terrence must be destroyed. I'm not asking you to harm them, but I am asking you not to get in the way of the humans.

"If they are not stopped, then the Lord of Chaos will be summoned. I know your people worshipped it in the past, but the thing about gods is that once they're walking the earth next to you, they're not at all what you expected them to be. I would rather not leave for school tomorrow with some other sorcerer causing this kind of mischief. It can't be one of my creations that are calling the demon. That's what is so confusing. It has to be one of yours or just some random wizard. But what are the odds of that? I wouldn't think any of your children beneath the lake would actually summon an ancient evil, at least not the sane ones. I hope you didn't create any psychos down there." He gave her a glare and she stared back at him. He sighed. "Anyway, I don't know what that cloaked figure is, but please do not get in the way of the humans, and if you get a chance to nab the bad wizard, please bring him or her back to me. I would love to find out why they would do something like this...if the humans don't kill them, of course."

The creature nodded, standing up and striding next to Cris.

"Make sure you're both back here before morning. We have a lot to do before we leave," the boy said, yawning and waving them away.

The two creatures rushed out of the cave and back into the water. After a short swim they came upon the bright light that shone through the trees and heard the faint, muttering curses of an ancient thing that made Cris very afraid. He turned his glassy stare to the female and she let out a fearful trill as well.

They crawled out of the lake and through the woods, approaching the clearing in the forest. The two of them stopped to hide behind two large trees. They peeked out at the hundreds of worm-faced demons housed inside human skin bags, and the Lord of Chaos shining from inside of a tree trunk. There was a low, growling voice buried deep beneath the earth...too deep to be heard clearly for now. Cris kept his eyes on the blackened trail and waited for the thing he loved.

Chapter 20

KATRINA REFUSED TO BELIEVE that Cris was dead. That thing underneath her arm was the leftover skin of some monster, but it wasn't her boyfriend. She just knew that he would be with Daisy, but when the muscular girl had come running down the trail gripping that huge gun, she was alone.

"You're alright!" Will said, squeezing Daisy tight.

"Where's Cris?" asked Billy as he finished his beer and threw it to the ground.

"I thought he was with you," Daisy said. "We got separated and I figured he went back down the trail. You didn't see him?"

Kat held out the skin suit with her head down. "We found this."

Daisy took it and spread the skin apart, examining the eyeless face. "Is that Cris?"

"No," Katrina said, snatching and folding the thing back up before sliding it under her arm again. "When did you see him last?"

"It was an hour or so ago. A bunch of snakes came barging down that trail and we both had to jump in the bushes. When I came out and yelled for him, he never answered. I looked and looked, and then made my way back here. He just disappeared."

"Did you get to the clearing?" asked the Professor.

"No, but I was constantly killing the oncoming traffic." Daisy removed the bloody baseball bat holstered over her back. "I probably knocked off a couple dozen heads with worms in them."

"How do you know one of them wasn't Cris?" Kat asked.

"I would have known, and I wouldn't have hurt him, Kat. You can tell who they are, even without the faces."

Katrina blew out a frustrated breath and started walking ahead alone.

"Where are you going?" asked Daisy.

Katrina didn't answer. She was going to find Cris and just knew he was in that clearing waiting for her.

"Let's get going," said Billy, following Kat with tears in his eyes.

They walked single file. Katrina was in front, followed closely by Billy. Daisy and Will trailed them a little, followed by the Professor. They walked together for almost an hour before Billy tapped Kat on the shoulder from behind.

"You want me to carry that for you?" he asked her, pointing to the skin suit.

"No," she said, gripping it tighter and turning around to face him. "It's not Cris, but I want to carry it anyway."

"Suit yourself," Billy said. "You're not the only one that's worried about him, you know. He's my son." He wiped his eyes. "If he's gone, I want you to know that he loved you very much and that I'm here for you, Kat."

Billy sniffled and hugged her.

Kat put an arm around him and held back tears of her own before replying. "Thanks, Billy. And he is still alive. He still loves us."

Billy let her go and they marched down the burnt trail.

"Professor?" Daisy asked while heading down the path fully loaded.

"Yes?"

"Have you noticed that we haven't seen any snakes yet?"

"Sure," he replied, "but I can hear them up ahead somewhere. Why?"

"It's just that there were tons of them at the entrance, and I can hear them up ahead too, but we've been walking for an hour and the noise just started to get a little louder. That means that we must have heard them from miles away. That's not possible, is it?"

"Not sure. They could have been moving ahead of us on the trail at a similar pace, or they could have been slithering along in the woods beside us. Or they could be heard from a hundred miles away, and that wouldn't surprise me in the least at this point. We're not dealing with natural phenomena anymore, Daisy, so anything is possible."

"Do you think all those people with worms in their faces will ever be able to go back to being normal again? Even after we kill Terrence?" asked Will.

"Maybe. I just don't know," the Professor said. "If the thing possessing Terrence is controlling all the worm-things in everyone else, then it might work. It would be kind of like cutting off the head to kill the body. If the thing in Terrence is the head, then the rest should die."

"Why aren't we being controlled too?" asked Daisy. "It seems like at least one of us should have been turned into one of those things."

He shrugged. "There's got to be some explanation. It can't just be a coincidence. There were other people with human faces still in town, so we weren't the only ones."

There was the sound of footsteps from behind and the Professor whirled to face another person approaching in the dark. He moved to the side, and as it passed they saw the two tiny yellow dots peering out of the darkness where there had once been a face. Daisy swung her weapon with a grunt, and those pinpricks fell to the ground.

"You alright, Professor?" Daisy asked, sheathing the bloody samurai sword.

He nodded, and both of them knelt down to look at the thing she had beheaded. Daisy pointed the flashlight at the face and the darkness was gone, replaced by Brother Pruitt.

"You killed the preacher, Daisy," said Will. "Holy shit! We're in a lot of trouble now."

"Just calm down, son," the Professor said while still kneeling down next to the thing. "It wasn't the pastor that she killed."

"Look!" Daisy pointed down as a fatty, grubby worm raced from behind the head and burrowed a hole into the trail. It moved so quickly that Daisy barely had time to stand and raise the sword above her head before it disappeared deep below the dirt, leaving a large hole in the ground. They heard it digging furiously somewhere down below and Daisy lowered the sword.

"Is it a worm?" Daisy asked.

"It was definitely worm-like," the Professor said, straining his head to look up ahead of them.

He bent back down and turned the pastor's head. There was a quarter-sized hole burrowed in the back of it. "Well, we know how the things exit," he said, standing up and dropping the head. "There's no time for an autopsy, so let's keep going."

The forest floor shook and they fell to the dirt. There was an unintelligible mumbling deep below them as the ground rumbled and then slowly grew still. The low mumbling speech continued after the movement subsided. The speech was old and coming from somewhere below, deep in the bowels of the earth. It was loud enough for them to make out that the same sounds were being repeated over and over again.

The Professor felt the muddy ground and lifted his hand to see it was covered in a thick red liquid. He saw the flowing blood. They got up with backsides soaked and stared at the steady stream of bodily fluids moving across the forest floor. It moved faster and faster, splashing over their shoes. The earth continued to mumble.

They walked the trail in silence, unable to hear anything except for the echoing, booming growl. They continued down the muddy trail and no one said a word. There was nothing to say. The evil voice below them was so loud by then, they couldn't have heard one another anyway.

The language made no sense to Kat, but she knew somehow that Brother Pruitt and all the others understood it. Daisy kept shining the flashlight on everyone, just to make sure they still had a face. They went farther and farther up the path as the blood slowed to a trickle and then stopped completely, but the groaning in the earth grew louder and louder.

Chapter 21

Fifty or so residents of Dalton County stood crowded together in the clearing. In front of this mass of people, a grinning Terrence gazed into the trunk of a tree. The base of the tree was overflowing with a bright yellow and green glow that illuminated all the people, and there was a faint moaning sound...a dark, deep, ancient growl that accompanied the light.

On one side of the trunk knelt a cloaked, hooded figure. On the other side was a cloaked boy with the hood down, silently mouthing words on his hands and knees. There were thousands of snakes hissing and wiggling across the ground.

Buddy stood inside the clearing, but more toward the back of the crowd. He could see everyone bathed in the light, but his field of vision was all screwed up. It was like he was looking through a pair of binoculars at something far away, and the black, widescreen-like borders of his sight were larger than the tiny screen that showed the world around him. He was looking out from somewhere deep inside himself, through alien eyes, and he had no control of his body.

The alien presence would occasionally move inside him, eliciting a slimy and disgusting disorientation. He prayed to Jesus that the thing would just sit still, but it kept moving anyway. Buddy could see enough of the scene outside himself to know that Terrence and that boy of his were up to no good. Something evil was in that tree, and it wanted out.

Buddy could still hear, but the noises were far away. All he heard at the moment was the hissing of snakes and the voice of the worm-like invader in his own head. Back at the preacher's pedophile park, the wriggling thing had burrowed itself in through his ear and marched his body into the woods. It had taken a while to get snug and comfortable in there. He had fought it at first, but Buddy had been pushed so far down by now that there was nothing to do but watch.

He watched the sea of snakes coalescing at one spot in the clearing, forming a waist-high mass of serpents climbing over each other. Then they moved toward the light and the deep, ancient growl got louder and louder until even Buddy could hear it pretty clearly. The snakes disappeared into the tree trunk and the blood began steadily pouring out. The reptile blood rushed past the standing, faceless humans and spread throughout the forest.

Buddy knew something evil was happening and wished he had never started stalking Terrence. He just wanted to be back at the trailer with his lover. He would give up all his security responsibilities for just one more chance to hold his sweet Lucille again. If he could somehow survive, that is what he would do. His days of risking life and limb for this community were over. He owed it to Lucille to retire and give her all the love and attention that she deserved.

He could live off his disability payments. Hell, it wasn't like the security gig actually paid anything. It was noble work, but he had a far nobler cause now: to get home to his fair maiden, bed her, and treat her properly for the rest of her days. He felt like crying, but that was beyond his control.

He could remember wandering through the woods for hours. It was like strings were attached to his body and pulling his legs up and letting go, pulling his arms this way and that. The invader was his puppet master, and his body obeyed its command, lumbering across the blackened trail and through the thick forest to the clearing. He could feel the power of the thing inside Terrence, as it controlled and commanded his own worm and all the others too. The evil presence in Terrence had gathered all of them together to watch this entity being birthed. Buddy didn't know what exactly the thing in the tree was, but he knew that it scared him.

The thing wriggled inside his skin and Buddy lost his wits and withdrew to his dark place. When it finally settled down, he heard it say something in worm-speak, and when the disorientation cleared, he saw the light glow brighter and smoke fill the forest. The blood was still splashing against his ankles, and the deep mumbling from the tree trunk was louder. Even though that voice was coming from far away, it drowned out all other sounds until he could no longer think of anything else. His mind went blank and Buddy just watched.

Cris and the female named Maggie stared with lidless eyes at the mass of humans. The duo saw the blood and the greenish-yellow light erupting, and they couldn't help but hear their ancient deity speaking loudly to them in a language they clearly understood. Cris now knew all about his people. The knowledge had been a part of him ever since the transformation.

It was a history that had been imprinted somehow in his new animal mind. He knew that Maggie and her species had flourished a long, long time ago in the lakes and rivers of the ancient world. They were killed for food, and back then they had no sorcerers among them to stop the humans. He knew that Maggie had gotten her magical gifts from the bald-headed boy that conjured her. She was essentially a witch, but her species had historically been nothing more than over-sized, carnivorous fish people.

They had fought back, stepping out of the water and onto the land, making new homes in the caves and islands. According to the history lesson in Cris's head, that had been their downfall. The humans waged war on them and their gods across the terra firma and destroyed their underwater homes. Their underground altars and structures were demolished, and the humans told tales of their war with the mer-people for many years until they devolved into nothing but fodder for fairy tales.

In a matter of months, Maggie had conjured up the whole civilization anew, but with magical powers like herself. They rebuilt the altars and prayed to the old gods once again. Apep had been one of those gods, and although Maggie loved all her race's deities, they were not responsible for summoning it. Cris sensed that she didn't know who was calling forth such evil, but they would soon find out.

He could tell that Maggie saw the bald boy as her father and would obey his every command. She had told him how the boy created her from his own mind, and she was now completely indebted to him. That hadn't always been the case though. She had acted without restraint for her first year of existence. But that was before she knew her creator, and now that she did, the female would guard his life for as long as the boy lived.

Maggie had created the other beings in her image. Being alone, and being a witch, the natural urge to create had spilled out of her. Before long, she had built a whole civilization with laws and leaders, and then quickly destroyed it and started over again when they became disobedient. She had given them too much free will, a mistake she did not make the second time around.

The creatures now living under the lake behaved, but she had grown tired of them and created a new leader to be their queen. This monarch had been ruling for months now and would be entrusted to rule them long after Maggie was gone.

All of these things and more, Cris somehow knew. Some of it he remembered as whispers from Maggie, but most of the information was just there, without being told to him or anything. It was as if the entire history of his people had been downloaded into his brain while he was on that algae gurney. Those eggs had been loaded with data that he was now accessing somehow.

The voice boomed in both of their heads, and Cris understood it clearly in a language he'd never heard spoken before. It beckoned both of them to come into the clearing and stand before the tree. This was the god of chaos, the god of all the creatures of darkness that hid in the shadows, and Cris was one of them now.

He had felt the urge to come to the clearing, but that wasn't really why he was there. Cris was there to protect the woman he loved from the dangerous monsters gathered together in the woods. He could tell that the calling was stronger with Maggie. However, even though the bonds to her ancestors were strong, her bond to the magician was stronger, and he knew she would not heed the call from the chaos god.

He tried to ignore the dark grumbling in his head and looked across the clearing. The boy to the side of the tree trunk was still silently moving his lips, but the hooded figure on the other side just knelt quietly and completely still. That mysterious figure never looked up and never moved. It wore a dark maroon cloak that covered every inch of its body with the hood up. The people were all faceless, but Cris could see the creatures within those voids and he wanted to eat them. He was starving.

He let out a little trill and Maggie trilled back. Then she rubbed her scaly nose against his shoulder in affection. She loved him like a child. Cris would have grinned if he could, but his mouth didn't work that way anymore. Instead, he looked at her for a moment with unblinking eyes and gaping mouth, before turning toward the trail to wait for Katrina.

The voice was very loud now, and it wasn't just speaking to him and Maggie, it was speaking to the entire world, or at least every living creature that understood it. All the monsters forced into hiding by the humans; all the monstrosities hunted almost to extinction; all the creatures forced into the shadows and underneath the earth or water; it was beckoning all of them to come...to come to Dalton County, Alabama, and follow the Lord of Chaos and Darkness.

Chapter 22

"Is that your real name or did you change it?" asked the elderly man behind the register.

"Real," Prince said in a soft voice, taking a pack of cigarettes from the cashier. "My mother had big plans for me."

"You ain't named for that pretty little singer?" asked the man. "You know, the skinny dead one?"

"No. She just loved the royal family. The look is my thing."

"Why?"

Prince shrugged. "It's what I want to see when I look in the mirror, I guess."

"Fair enough," said the old man, waving his hand.

Prince Pointer walked out of the gas station and sat on a bench outside. He lit a cigarette and watched the occasional headlights fly past in the dark. While he smoked, a family from two states over pulled up to the fuel pump. As the man got out and pumped gas into their little fuel-efficient compact car, the driver looked around the parking lot suspiciously.

His eyes fell on the greasy-haired little man in dark purple leather and a pink headband. Prince smiled at him, but the man did not smile back. He finished pumping and shot a disgusted glance at Prince. The tires squealed as the vehicle raced away.

Once the family moved on, Prince stomped out the cigarette and strode over to his Harley Davidson. He put on the black skullcap, and then the black helmet over that. He caught the cashier watching him through the glass door. His face had been all over the news. By now, anyone with a television might recognize him. The motorcycle engine roared to life, and he peeled out of the gas station and onto the open road.

When the Professor left earlier that night, he gave Prince explicit instructions to stay in the room and not to sit on the recliner. If not for the Professor, he would most likely be in prison for the rest of his life. In the future, he would do whatever the man said, but this one time he had to disobey in order to help. Prince just knew, deep in his gut, that they needed his help. He had a part to play in this plan, whether the wizard realized it or not.

After the Professor was gone, Prince had sat on the rug and watched the tiny heads floating in the jars of liquid. One of the little goblin heads was so monstrous and creepy that it made him remember why he had joined the Ghost Raiders in the first place. Since they were teenagers, he and Charlie had wanted to discover things just like that screaming face in the jar, and now all kinds of supernatural things were happening in the woods nearby.

Prince knew the Professor wasn't in any mortal danger. The man couldn't die—not for good, at least. But he felt so helpless just sitting on that rug. He wanted more than anything to be a part of the adventure, to see the things that other people would never know even existed. Things like that evil priest that killed the man he had loved. Of course, his friend had never felt that way toward him, but Prince couldn't help who he fell in love with. He had loved two girlfriends and a boyfriend, and they were all dead now. He knew that if Charlie could speak from wherever people went when they died, his friend would tell Prince to go to the woods and see the things they had only dreamed of seeing as kids.

There were no other cars on the road to the lake. He passed miles and miles of houses with their porch lights off and several closed gas stations, but other than that it was nothing but dark wilderness on both sides of the road. He crossed a little bridge and saw the Baptist church on the right. There were shadowy figures walking aimlessly through the front yard. It was the first people he had seen since the gas station.

He flew by the church and saw the little graveyard next to it crowded with people too. When he turned his head back to the road, there was a rotted corpse with no arms standing in the middle of it.

Prince swerved to the left, barely avoiding impact with the thing, before veering back into the correct lane. He slowed down and turned the bike around in the middle of the road, shining the headlights on the mass of corpses now stumbling across the road.

Over the rumble of the idle engine, he could hear a voice muttering gibberish that he couldn't understand from somewhere far away. It was a low, muffled speech and it was coming from deep in the woods. Rotted men in suits moved slowly toward the bridge before descending a pathway that led down to the lake. The whole zombie horde soon followed, moving slowly in the general direction of the voice.

The dead people seemed harmless enough. Prince started to turn the bike around when he saw something way too big and moving way too fast to be a dead thing. A gigantic, hairy creature rushed across the street, shoving one of the dead people to the ground. It was over seven feet tall, ape-like, and swung two long, powerful arms as it ran. The Bigfoot turned its head slightly toward the little man on the bike, seeming to acknowledge him for a moment before stepping down the pathway to the lake.

He gunned the engine, racing the last two miles to the lake entrance. Prince needed to get to the Professor quickly if he was going to be of any help. Before leaving the barn, he remembered taking one last look at that empty chair in the secret room and realizing that his mentor would appear there eventually, but his new friends were in danger too, and there was only one recliner. If the group failed, then this god-like entity would rain chaos and destruction down on the world, and even the secret room may not be safe for them anymore. And from the looks of the church he just passed, that rain had already started.

He saw the cars parked on the side of the road as the bike pulled into the park. Prince slowed down to zigzag through the chaos of abandoned vehicles. Somewhere near the picnic area, he sat on his bike and surveyed the park.

A trail was clearly visible on one side, but he took a moment to gather himself before approaching that tunnel in the woods. He didn't see any zombies in the picnic area, but he figured they were headed in the direction of the low, guttural voice that he still heard over the idling engine of the bike.

The Professor warned him about the dangers of leaving the house, but Prince was sure he hadn't meant things like this. He was an escaped convict now, a murderer in the eyes of the public. If anyone alive recognized his face from the news, they wouldn't hesitate to call the police, or even shoot him and try to carry him in themselves. He wasn't sure what was more dangerous, the humans or the stumbling corpses.

Prince removed the helmet and put it on his lap. He pulled out a cigarette and lit it with a long-handled lighter. He had never really been a heavy smoker, but that was before he became an outlaw. The engine idled and his lungs filled with smoke. One hand tapped the gallon container of gasoline strapped to the rear of the bike. If the world thought he was a dangerous man, then he would give them one.

A creature howled in the night. Prince heard a splash in the lake and did a double take at what he thought he saw in the darkness. He pointed the bike's headlights that way to get a better look. There was an enormous mass jutting out of the water, and when the headlights were upon it, he could see that it was alive.

Only the square head of the monster was exposed, with everything below the mouth still underneath the lake. It was like a large island in the water, with one monstrous eye that moved slowly back and forth in the middle of it. The mouth was a closed slit, but the night was filled with the sound of its heavy breathing, and then the ground shook violently.

Whoosh!

Whoosh!

The sound of huge wings flapping above the forest made him look away from the great cyclopic Kraken in the lake. His head tilted upward in time to see the outline of a winged beast gliding over the trees. An echoing growl erupted from the bird-like thing, and he looked back at the water to see the gigantic island rising even higher above the lake.

He couldn't help but feel alien eyes upon him from all directions. There were howling, guttural moans and all manner of inhuman sensations in those woods and beyond. They all seemed to be moving in the same direction he was headed.

He put on his helmet and threw the cigarette in the grass. Gunning it, the loud motorcycle engine blocked out most of the monstrous sounds as he roared through the picnic area and barreled down the trail. The headlights shone just a few feet ahead as he blasted through the forest like a rocket ship. The pathway got narrower and narrower, but there was just enough room for his Harley. The gas container sloshed behind him, and the machete hanging from his belt dangled off the side of the seat. There was something mysterious and danger-ous happening at the end of that trail, and underneath his helmet, the little man grinned.

Chapter 23

"DAMNED THINGS WON'T DIE," Daisy said, raising the dripping wet baseball bat and swinging at a corpse.

The rotten head flew from the suited torso, smacking a tree with a wet thud. Daisy swung downward at the open neck of the now headless thing, smashing it to the ground. The creature was stunned, but after a moment the broken body sat up on all fours and crawled past her, zigzagging down the path in quick, jerky motions like an over-sized insect.

"I don't think we can destroy them all," the Professor said, glaring down the trail to see more movement headed their way. "We need to outrun them. They all seem to be going to the same place."

The Professor quickly moved out of the way as a headless corpse brushed by him, swinging something at its side. Will stood firm on the trail and swung the sledgehammer sideways at the thing, hitting its arm and sending the body flailing into the woods. Something fell out of the creature's hand as it flew off the trail. It was a severed head, and when it landed upright, the eyes snapped open.

"It's that preacher," Daisy said. "Kill it!"

The preacher head opened its gaping mouth just as the sledgehammer connected, crunching the skull down the middle. It continued writhing and biting on air, so Will pulled out the hammerhead and kicked the nasty thing into the woods.

Will grabbed Daisy's arm. "Come on, honey. You'll get to kill plenty of things when we make it to the clearing. For now, we just got to keep moving. There's no telling what else is coming up that path."

"You're a hot little thing, you know that?" Daisy said with a smile before kissing him square on the mouth.

The three of them ran past the crawling, headless zombie. Daisy gave it one last kick in the gut as she went by. They almost ran into Billy and Kat, who were standing in the path, staring into the darkness above.

Daisy touched Katrina's arm, which was still clutching the skin suit, and spoke softly to her. "What's going on, Kat? What you looking at?"

"You didn't hear it?" asked Katrina.

"The huge wings flapping overhead," Billy said, still looking up and straining his eyes. "I caught a glimpse as it passed over. The wings were massive, Albert. Like a dinosaur or something."

The Professor moved past Daisy and shook his brother-in-law by the shoulders. "Billy! Look at me!"

Billy looked down and made eye contact with Albert.

"There are dead people coming down the trail," the Professor said.

"Zombies?" asked Billy.

"Yes, and we have to keep moving since there are lots and lots of them moving this way and this path is very thin." The Professor tilted his head up and then back to Billy again. "Forget about the bird. We've got our own problems down here."

Billy nodded and finished his beer, throwing the can into the woods. "You see anything else coming our way?"

"Other than zombies? Isn't that enough?" asked Will.

"Well, yeah," Billy said, "but we saw that winged thing, and heard some noises like water splashing. It sounded pretty big too."

There was a howling from not so far away, followed by a low growl.

"What was that?" asked Will.

"Sounded like a wolf," said the Professor, shrugging. "Probably a werewolf, the way this night is going."

"A werewolf?" asked Daisy.

Suddenly, a giant shadow covered them all in darkness as something huge raced past them through the thick wood. They turned quick enough to see a shape almost as tall as the trees. It was moving so quickly that it vanished in seconds, but an echoing growl continued a few moments after it was gone.

"That was too large to be a werewolf," the Professor said.

There was another growl, and they all looked into the forest ahead to see another giant, shadowy shape moving through the trees before disappearing into the darkness.

"There's no telling, but they sure are big," Daisy said. "We heard the water splashing too, but whatever's in the water is too far away to worry about right now. We've got to get to that clearing, and fast."

Moans and grunts were approaching from behind as they marched up the trail in a single-file line. Billy let Daisy lead the way. The Professor stayed at the back of the line, and as they moved up the path, he could hear the dead giving chase.

However, the Professor was too deep in thought to worry about a dusty old corpse snatching him from behind. He was formulating a plan. He had to figure out the best way to die and take Terrence with him, and he had to do so before something killed him unexpectedly.

He thought about a smash and grab job. Just running up and shooting the possessed man in the head, and if the creatures killed him afterward, then so be it. However, there was a chance, a good chance, that a bullet in the head wouldn't kill the thing inside Terrence. So he had to plan something much more destructive than that. There was always fire, but he had been an idiot and not taken the gasoline from the shed. They had plenty of guns and sharp objects, but the Professor really wished he had brought a hand grenade or something.

Cutting off the head seemed like the best available tactic, but he would need Daisy's sword to do that. He could get it from her and take off running into the clearing, chop off the head, and then keep chopping Terrence up until it finally killed him. They had guns, and he figured they could use them on the other monsters, but there were just too many unanswered questions to properly formulate a good plan.

The main question that had been bothering him the whole trip was why none of them had become worm faces. Also, there was the issue of why the Jenkins boy didn't just do some type of magic and fix everything himself.

And why had I brought that stupid screwdriver?

"We're here," Daisy whispered from up ahead.

Everyone stopped. She put one finger over her mouth, and with the other she pointed to a couple of especially large trees in the woods to the left of the path. The group moved quietly behind them and watched as the zombie horde clumsily passed where they had just been.

They could see the clearing from a spot behind the two large trees that were so close to one another they almost touched. There were dozens of worm-faced people crammed together, and even more silhouetted in the dark forest on the other side. The zombies were standing restlessly in the trail and spilling into the clearing, pushing their way through the possessed humans.

On one end, Terrence stood in front of the tree trunk, basking in the bright yellow-green light that emitted from inside. The low, ancient sounds echoed out of the tree as he stood with arms outstretched, silently moving his lips in unison with the booming voice.

To one side of the trunk was a cloaked boy with his hood down. The child was seated on his knees, entranced and mumbling with eyes closed. To the other side of the glowing tree was a figure in a dark maroon cloak seated on the earth. The head was down, but it suddenly lifted, and the Professor gasped. It was a caricature of someone he recognized vaguely, but couldn't quite remember who it reminded him of. The yellow glow on that gaunt, bony countenance resembled a fleshless skull more than any flesh and blood person.

The Professor blinked and the figure was gone. He looked across the clearing for him, and his eyes fell on the giant black knight named Reginald, who was solemnly watching the proceeding. The Jenkins boy was asleep on the creature's chest in a large baby carrier, snug as a bug. He figured the wizard had to be under some sort of spell to be sleeping on a night like this. Maybe the child had put a spell into motion already, but there was no way to find out at the moment. The boy wizard was incapacitated, and the Professor was on his own.

He noticed that Reginald was staring directly at him. The knight awkwardly lifted an arm, giving a half-assed sort of embarrassed wave as he politely flapped a gloved hand back and forth a few times. The Professor scowled at the knight and then politely raised a hand back in acknowledgment.

Behind the armored gentleman, huge shadows moved in the darkness. Some seemed taller than the tallest trees. Their snarls could be heard over the deep muttering of the thing in the tree trunk. From their shadows it seemed the things had lots of thin legs and moved very fast.

The flapping of giant wings whooshed above the trees. A deafening series of croaks came from the far end of the clearing, where a gigantic toad towered over the possessed humans. Its huge, flabby body fluttered with each booming, wet sound that erupted from its mouth. The toad's bulging eyes scanned the clearing, moving back and forth. Every time it glared their way, the Professor and all his companions tried to hide behind the tree, not daring to make eye contact with that awful amphibian.

Once the disgustingly giant toad turned away, the Professor leaned out from behind the tree again and saw all manner of creatures outlined in the darkness of the woods beyond the clearing. There were ululating cries erupting from the other side, and the sound of heavy breathing all around. They kept looking behind them, but so far nothing had approached or seemed to mind them too much at all. It seemed that all the creatures except for the toad were too enraptured by what was in the base of the tree to even notice them.

The cloaked thing with the glowing skull face was back, seated on one side of the trunk, with the cloaked boy seated on the other side. They both seemed to be concentrating awfully hard. The Professor remembered what the client had said about the Boogeyman, the maroon-cloaked figure that would come into their room during the night and mutter incantations in the dark. He quickly figured that Boogeyman may be behind this portal in the tree trunk.

He could tell it was a portal or doorway for other creatures to come through, because every so often something moved inside it against the light. He could feel the Lord of Chaos on the other side. More and more monsters would be coming their way, and if the entity was summoned into the clearing, then Apep could spread this army of acolytes, and humans wouldn't stand a chance.

While trying to come up with a plan, he saw two of the worm-faced townspeople carrying a young boy by the hands and feet. They placed the child in front of the trunk and slit his throat. The blood spurted then flowed from his neck as the two possessed humans dumped the dying boy against the base of the tree.

One of them grabbed a headful of hair and pulled the head back, opening up the wound so the blood poured onto the wood. The light grew brighter. The muttering boomed a little louder, and all the creatures in the forest got a little more excited. Four more children were dragged to the trunk and killed. Each time, the light grew brighter and the booming voice got louder.

The Professor noticed Billy staring at him.

"We've got to do something," Billy whispered. "They just killed five of those abducted kids, for God's sake."

The Professor nodded and looked to see Will, Daisy, and Kat staring at him too. All of them were awaiting an ingenious plan that did not exist. He considered the options for a moment, then whispered to them.

"I think we've got to stop the two cloaked figures from chanting. I think they might be wizards and are probably keeping the portal open." The Professor sighed. "I know we have to stop that evil muttering thing from coming through, and they seem the most likely options for having opened it. Daisy, you and Will cut a path toward the tree. Kat and Billy, you go to the boy and shut him up."

"You want us to kill him?" asked Billy.

"No," the Professor whispered. "At least not if you don't have to. Just slap him around a little bit or something. Daisy, you and Will go after the Boogeyman...I mean, the maroon-cloaked figure by the tree. You can kill him if you want."

Daisy grinned.

"I'm going to take out Terrence," Albert said, holding up the screwdriver, "but I can't very well cut his head off with this."

He looked at Daisy.

"Oh," Daisy said, pulling out her samurai sword and handing it over.

"Thanks," whispered the Professor, holding the sword. "You just go in guns a-blazing and I'll be right behind you. Remember, cut off all the heads, except for the boy. I got a feeling the Boogeyman is making him do it, so let's try not to take off the child's head if we can help it."

The muttering from the tree trunk was so loud now that they could no longer hear the other creatures in the forest. Daisy locked and loaded the automatic weapon and nodded.

Will stood behind her, gripping his sledgehammer.

Billy held the hoe tightly with both hands.

Katrina gripped a small hatchet in one hand and clutched the skin suit with the other.

The Professor held the shiny blade in front of his chest.

"Ready?" the Professor whispered to the group. "Let's go."

BOOM!

BOOM!

The creatures all turned their attention to the gunfire as Daisy rushed into the clearing with guns blazing. She screamed and exploded the worm-faced heads and zombies in her way. She managed to make a pathway, but more swarmed closer and closer around them.

When Daisy reached Terrence, she grabbed Will's hand and darted to the side with the maroon-cloaked figure.

Kat and Billy darted to the other side, leaving the Professor staring up at the possessed yellow eyes of Terrence.

Approaching the kneeling person, Daisy threw down her gun and pulled the Louisville Slugger from the sling on her back. She swung at the head, but hit nothing but air and fell onto the empty maroon cloak that was now bundled on the ground where the figure had once knelt.

Daisy looked frantically around her, but only saw dozens of menacing eyes in the dark woods.

The Boogeyman had vanished.

Billy approached the cloaked boy, rearing back and slapping him across the face. The boy fell to the side. His hood fell back and the child rubbed his bruised face. His lips stopped moving and he looked confused.

"Hey," the boy said, startled out of whatever trance he had been in. "Where am I?"

"Stay still!" Billy said, glaring down at the boy. "What is it you were muttering anyway?"

"Muttering? I don't know." The boy looked around confused. His eyes widened and his lip quivered. "Are those zombies?"

"There are worse things than zombies, son," Billy said. "Just stay put. Your sister hired us to rescue you."

"Thanks," the boy said, his eyes slowly moving from monster to monster.

The man who was once Terrence grinned like a madman with the bright light shining from behind. The worm faces crowded in closer.

The Professor gulped as the booming voice lessened a little, and the greenish-yellow light grew just a shade darker. A surprised Terrence turned his head toward the tree. When he turned it back, the sword was swinging at his neck. The possessed man ducked, and the weight of the blade took the Professor to the ground.

"Brave little wizard," Terrence said, standing over him. "I do not need their incantations anymore. The spell is cast and you are too late. Our Lord is here."

The Professor swung his head to see a black tentacle as wide around as the tree flop out of the trunk and hit the ground. Dozens of hissing snake heads protruded from the glistening, wet appendage. It was the black of burnt flesh and still steaming.

At the end of the tentacle was the tiny, round face of a human with a thin-lipped smile and eyes closed. A small blue fire ignited below the weird face, and a roar shook everything, including the forest floor.

The roar ceased and the Professor gathered himself to see Terrence staring in awe at his recently summoned Master. He located the samurai sword on the ground, but instead of reaching for it, he remembered the screwdriver. The Professor gripped the flat-headed tool in both hands and brought it down hard, straight through Terrence's foot and into the dirt.

As the possessed man turned, the Professor stood with the sword raised and swung it as hard as he could. The head fell to the ground and the yellow eyes flipped open.

Terrence's head grinned up at him.

The light from the tree did not diminish and the headless body remained standing, spurting blood out of the neck hole. It stuck out an arm and pointed an index finger emphatically at the man in the lab coat, while the head on the ground continued smiling in silence.

The worm-faced people moved out of the way as dozens of zombies lumbered through the crowd. They held the Professor by the arms and legs before forcing him to the ground and ripping his belly open with their bare hands. As they tore out his intestines, the Professor rolled his eyes and sighed heavily, and then woke up alone in the recliner.

Chapter 24

KATRINA STOOD NEXT TO Billy and dropped her hatchet on the ground. She wasn't going to murder the boy. He wasn't even muttering spells anymore, and she wasn't going to murder anyone else. Kat's shoulders slumped forward as she tightened her armpit around the skin suit and stopped fighting.

She was surrounded by monsters and knew there was no way she was ever getting out of the forest alive. Katrina wondered why she had gone out here in the first place, before remembering how excited she had been chasing after monsters with Cris. She had never seriously considered they might die. Not really. It had all been kind of fun and games until...until he left her all alone. Now it was a nightmare, and she just wanted it over.

Billy had a gardening tool, for God's sake. She was standing next to a sobbing boy in an oversized cloak while a giant tentacle of biting snakes was being birthed into this world from the inside of a tree trunk. She could barely make out Daisy and Will across the bright illumination erupting from the base of the tree, but they would soon be dead too.

Daisy had pumped the tree trunk full of lead and Will had bashed it with a sledgehammer, but no bark flew off and it was not harmed at all. It wasn't a natural thing, and any idiot could tell you that bullets and metal weren't going to do any good against ancient evil entities or the trees they crawled out of.

Terrence had been decapitated, but it seemed that the process had reached a point of no return and the thing in the portal was still coming out. Daisy and Will were still trying to chop and hammer their way to Terrence, who now palmed his own head to one side, but the creatures had created a wall of protection around their leader. The lips on the severed head mouthed the final incantations and the eyes were wide open. Blood poured from the neck hole, joining the large puddle of bodily fluids on the dirt. Several zombies were currently lapping it up with their bony hands.

It was a nightmare, and Katrina just wanted the terror to end. She had watched as the Professor decapitated Terrence and then ran off into the woods. She couldn't blame him for running, though, since the headless body just picked up the grinning face and went on with his evil work. Apparently, they had not brought destructive enough weaponry. Even if Daisy and Will got to Terrence, all they could do was put holes in him or smash him a few times with the hammer before the creatures overran them.

Kat watched the swarm of monsters as a second tentacle emerged from the trunk. It was much larger than the first, and she had to look up to see the gigantic sharp-toothed mouth of a cobra dangling in the air at the end of the appendage. The hood surrounding the fangs flared outward, and the entire glistening tentacle was covered in tiny fanged mouths.

Katrina caught a glimpse of something above the cobra head and looked past it to see the silhouette of four large winged things that looked like giant bats, flapping their huge muscles and blocking the stars from view. Tears fell from her eyes and she giggled hysterically. She glanced over to see Billy's frightened face, and that made her laugh even more. The zombies and worm-faced creatures in her vicinity ignored her, completely transfixed by the birth of the ancient one.

Katrina was snorting with asylum laughter, eyes wet and closed, when suddenly she had the breath knocked out of her. The impact knocked her to the ground at the edge of the clearing. She felt her head pound against something hard and the world went fuzzy. She managed to roll over and saw a fish-face staring down at her...a fish face with gentle eyes. The corners of its large lips seemed to move upward, and she couldn't help but smile back at the creature in her maddened state. It had the face of a fish, but the body was more reptilian, like a lizard, all scaly with a thick tail. The creature stood on two legs, staring down at her for only a moment, before she heard the whoosh of flames followed by a loud BOOM!

Everything was so blurry, but she could make out the flames, and the last thing she saw was that fish face towering over her before everything went completely dark.

Prince saw the bodies up ahead and honked the horn. The zombies turned and jumped out of the way as the speeding motorcycle flew past. He hadn't figured they would just move out of the way like that and was making good time.

On the ride up the trail, he had formulated a plan. Prince had taken off his scarf and jammed it into the nozzle of the gasoline container now fitted into place on his lap. He planned to use the scarf as a fuse and set everything on fire. This seemed like an excellent plan considering he really didn't know what to expect when he got to the clearing, and even if they couldn't die, most things could burn.

There would be walking dead since they were everywhere. Also, he had been told about a man named Terrence that seemed to be the leader of the evil things, so it was a yellow-eyed man with a goblin chin that he was looking to light up first.

When he reached the clearing, Prince had no problem locating Terrence. The body that stood in front of the glowing tree trunk with tentacles flopping out of it held a head with a pointed chin and yellow eyes.

Prince gunned the bike.

He leaned to one side and gripped the container to let the bike slide away from his legs and fall sideways to the ground. The motorcycle's momentum carried the bike on its side toward the possessed man, who stepped out of the way to let it tear a path along the side of the tree.

Prince saw the people from the barn and yelled, "Get away from the tree!" as loud as he could while the bike was still sliding across dirt.

He saw a giant fish-man knock Kat out of the way of the oncoming motorcyle. The others moved quickly away from the tree and into the woods.

Prince lit the scarf and rushed toward the tree, using his body to shield the fuse. He placed the container on the ground next to the tree, and as the fuse burnt farther down, he raced to the edge of the woods before the explosion propelled him airborne into the brush.

Prince stood up and saw the flaming body still clutching the head of Terrence, and then it crumpled to the ground. There were zombies on fire, clumsily lumbering around catching everything they touched ablaze. Many of the worm-faced people were burning too. He watched as their countenance transformed from the worm-filled void to the faces of his neighbors.

The fish-faced thing stomped out into the clearing and looked in Prince's general direction. It had the eternally surprised countenance of a trout, but from the neck down it was a two-legged, scaly beast. Three lightly toasted zombies were approaching the creature from behind, but it didn't seem to notice as its head moved back and forth, frantically searching for someone it couldn't find. The tiny man in leather wanted to yell at the monster to look out, but was still unsure whose side it was on.

Just as the dead bodies reached the creature's back, another giant fish-faced thing stepped into the clearing. One at a time, the newcomer palmed each zombie's head, plucked it from their shoulders, and tossed them to the ground. The dead bodies still walked aimlessly into the first creature, but the newly arrived one shoved them and they flew a good ten feet in the air. The headless things hit the ground and then fled into the woods, barreling into trees and blindly scurrying out of sight.

When Prince looked back, the two creatures were gone. He watched as the magical glow of the tree trunk dissipated and the yellow-green light was replaced with the red and orange of a gasoline fire. He noticed the gas tank of his motorcycle was in close proximity to the trunk. Prince got a few steps farther away from the clearing before a second explosion, more powerful than the first, erupted. A small mushroom cloud of fire bellowed upward, and everything was shrouded in a thick veil of smoke.

When the fog cleared, he couldn't see any sign of the serpent tentacles that were there just moments ago. There were two dozen or so burning figures shambling around, shrieking in pain.

He saw Terrence on fire, still holding his flaming head.

Almost everything in the clearing was on fire. Most of the burning dead either screamed or flailed around until their body became too weak to support itself and fell to the ground.

The trees that had been crowded were now almost completely empty of monsters. Just about everything that had responded to the call of the ancient evil had crawled back into the shadows once again.

The giant shadowy beasts had vanished.

The worm-faced things were people now.

The entire tree was on fire, and whatever summoning had taken place was now over.

In the woods on the other side of the clearing, he could barely make out the thick, scaly back of what looked like one of the two-legged fish creatures. It was running—more like a long striding hop from one leg to another—carrying something in its arms like a bundle of twigs. It only took a second or two for it to disappear into the darkness.

As Prince's vision came back to the clearing, he saw two huge amphibious eyes, the eyes of a frog that was taller than he was, staring directly at him. He did a double take, but when he looked a second time, it was gone too.

He looked up and there were no winged creatures above the trees, only a sky full of stars. A muscle-bound girl holding a bloody baseball bat walked out from behind a tree alongside a Ken doll with a sledge-hammer. They entered the clearing, followed shortly by the drunk from the barn. Prince slid behind a large tree and spied on them.

"Katrina!" yelled Daisy, stepping over a burning body.

"Kat!" yelled Billy. "Albert! Did you see where Albert went?"

Daisy shook her head. "Not really. He just took off running through the woods. That huge scaly thing picked Kat up and went that way. I'm going after her. Will, you and Billy stay here for now."

She rushed into the woods as Will and Billy stood over the burning Terrence corpse and stared down at it.

"You think it's dead?" asked Will.

Billy kicked the blackened, fiery skull, and the whole burnt, ashy body collapsed in a puff of smoke. "It looks dead to me, and that weird portal in the tree is gone too. So I guess we stopped it somehow."

"What was that cobra-looking monster coming out of it?" asked Will. "Was that the Apep thing you were talking about?"

Billy nodded. "Yeah. I always thought it would be a really tall monstrosity on two legs, or it would take some form that was more human-like. I didn't expect it to be an actual snake."

Will looked at the tree. "That was just one head. There was the other one too. The eyes never opened on that face, but I saw the corners of the mouth moving around."

"I saw that," said Billy, shifting uncomfortably. "Hell, it could have eventually come out on two legs for all I know. I'm just glad we didn't get a chance to see it. At least the monster mash is over."

Will nodded and looked around at the people. Some of the towns-folk were seated on the dirt rubbing their heads, while others were dead, their burnt bodies lying on the earth.

"All of them seem to have their faces back," Will said.

Billy spat. "Yup. I see some of the Stoddard family still breathing over there. Lucky bastards. I've got half a mind to burn them up before the cops come. Did you see where that little guy went off to? Maybe he's got some more gasoline."

"I don't know why he flew in here blowing up shit, but that little guy's an escaped killer. He's dangerous."

"Hell yeah he is." Billy said. "Murderer or not, though, he sure saved our asses."

Prince turned and started walking quietly through the woods. He pushed through the brush deeper and deeper into the forest, following alongside the trail from far enough away where people coming up it wouldn't see him.

There was a chance he could have sneaked into the clearing and got his bike if he waited around for the two men to leave, but the previously possessed citizens were already getting up. Not only that, but the police were sure to be swarming pretty soon, with all the explosions and forest fires. The bike would have to be left for now, and he needed to head down that trail if he was going to stay out of prison.

As the little man waded through the thorns and weeds, he heard the rustling sounds of people approaching up the trail and looked over to see the police speeding down, with flashlights and guns drawn. He moved farther into the deep woods, away from the trail, trying to get to the highway as quickly as possible.

His leather clothes were soaked through with sweat, and he was still coming down from the adrenaline rush. The man was exhausted and knew his body would crash soon.

Prince thought about the zombie horde and all the creatures in the woods earlier that night, and he realized just how alone he really was. With Charlie gone, what family he had left didn't care whether he lived or died. Sure, he loved his mother, but she had never really loved him back. At least, that's what she told him. Charlie had been his only real family, and now it seemed there was no one left alive that cared for him anymore.

Prince didn't know what time it was when he saw the picnic area and flashing police lights up ahead. Luckily, the sun was still down enough for him to sneak along the lake front and onto the bridge without being noticed. From there, it was a mile walk before he had cell phone service again.

The stars were losing their battle with the rising sun when he finally put the phone to his ear. There was an open gas station up ahead and he sat down in the corner of the parking lot and lit up a cigarette.

The phone rang four times before someone answered.

"Hello?"

"Professor?" asked Prince, tears of relief and exhaustion forming in his eyes. "Is that really you?"

"Yes, son. It's really me. Now, tell me where you are so I can bring you home."

Chapter 25

Katrina woke as the sun came up, and the first thing she saw on the ground next to her was the skin suit. She slapped her arm, then head, feeling ants crawling over her entire body. Kat stood up quickly and began rubbing and hitting her skin, trying to kill or knock off all the insects.

"Katrina?"

She turned to see a smiling Daisy move out from behind a large tree.

"You alright, Kat?"

"I think so," Katrina replied, picking up Cris's skin and giving her friend a hug.

"It's over, Kat," Daisy said, hugging her tight before letting go and looking around nervously. "Did that thing carry you out here? Is it gone?"

"I think it saved my life. When it was carrying me away, I heard the explosions. I think it was protecting me. I know it was Daisy. I could see it in his eyes. Those eyes were so kind, and so familiar."

"Well, it's gone now," Daisy said. "I think we should get you to the hospital."

"But I'm fine."

Kat followed Daisy's eyes downward to the blood-soaked pants leg that stuck to the wet wound underneath.

"You're not fine," Daisy said. "Besides the leg, you got some burns on your arms and face that need treated too. You must have been closer to the explosions than us. We started running when we saw that murderer flying in on his motorcycle. That little dude saved our ass. I can't believe none of us thought to bring some gasoline."

"Is Prince alright?" asked Kat.

Daisy shrugged, motioning for Kat to follow her as she moved through the woods. "He disappeared. The cops are out there with the dogs trying to find him. They stopped me as I was looking for you and didn't believe a word I said about what happened. They just looked at me like I was crazy when I told them about the portal, about Terrence and the monsters."

"I guess we've got to come up with a story that doesn't include demonic possession and tentacled things from beyond," Katrina said while trying to keep up with her friend.

"Nah, I think the cops already got their story. They were more interested in Prince, especially when I told them about him starting the fire. However, once I figured out they weren't going to believe me, I conveniently left out the part about the Professor chopping off Terrence's head and about any worm-faced heads we might have removed."

"Good idea," Kat said. "Are they all still possessed like that?"

"The ones that survived the burning are back to normal now, no worms or nothing, but they don't remember shit. That's the problem. We're the only ones that remember anything, and what we saw was unbelievable. So the police are crafting their own more natural story-line at the moment. They think the fire killed everyone that's dead, so they're looking to pin several dozen more murders on that little guy."

Kat followed Daisy into the clearing and saw the smoke, the smoldering ash, and the police officers standing around with flashlights.

Some of the officers were interviewing people, while others were standing around smoking cigarettes. There was police tape around the clearing, and Daisy lifted it up for the two to step underneath.

They hurried through the fiery mess to the trail on the other side. There were uniformed officers all along the pathway. Kat saw Officer Turner coming toward them and she quickly stuffed the skin bag underneath her shirt.

"I see you found Katrina," the officer said, before noticing the huge bump on her head and the bloody leg. "Whoa, why don't you get on Harvey's bike."

Officer Turner waved at another cop, who wheeled a motorcycle around as the pathway cleared for his approach. Over the rumbling motor, Turner pointed to Katrina, and the officer on the motorbike patted the cushion behind him.

"Kat!"

She turned and saw her dad running their way. He hugged her hard and she hugged him back. Before Katrina could help it, she was crying into his shoulder and he was stroking her hair, just like she was a little girl again.

"It's alright," he whispered to her. "Everything's gonna get better. I promise."

She stopped crying and opened her eyes to see her mom and her little brother, Randall, standing with hands in his pockets. He smiled at her and she smiled back. Then everything went blurry for a moment and her dad caught her before she fell backward to the ground.

"Whoa," Officer Turner said. "Your daughter's lost a lot of blood, Mr. Thompson. We really need to get her to the hospital."

"Kat," her dad said, holding her up by the shoulders. "You still with me?"

She opened her eyes and the world faded into view. "Yeah. Yeah, I'm alright."

Her father helped Katrina onto the bike and she wrapped her arms around Officer Harvey's flabby waist. The bike moved away and she turned to see her little brother and parents waving at her briefly, and then they disappeared.

The bike moved slowly down the trail at first, dodging the mass of civilians and officers on the narrow path. She watched as everyone moved out of the way.

There was Buddy talking to an officer. He smiled and nodded at her.

She saw the faces of the Stoddard boys and their scowling mother with a burning cigarette dangling from her mouth.

Soon they passed pretty much everyone, and Officer Harvey sped up. The two of them raced down the path for what seemed like forever. The whole way she kept looking into the woods on either side of her for a pair of eyes, but even as the sun came up completely, she saw no one out there.

She couldn't figure out why that monster had saved her. Perhaps it had been watching them all along and somehow knew where Cris was. If only she could ask it a question or two, maybe get a clue as to where he might be.

The wind scattered her tears, and Kat realized she would never see Cris again.

"I told you what I saw," Buddy said to the police officer as they stood on the trail together. "I woke up from a trance and saw a guy on fire holding his head in one hand. There were zombies, and I saw some type of giant frog staring at me too. It felt like I was possessed by something, and I think I saw everything that was going on, but now I can't remember much. It was like that body snatchers book."

"You mean the movie?" asked the officer, who was in his early twenties and puffing on a cigarette.

"Well, I guess like the movie too, but I read the book when I was little."

"Didn't know there was a book." The officer scribbled some things down. "So, did you see this Prince person fly in on the motorcycle and light up the place?"

"Nope. When I woke up, he must have been gone. I never saw the creep."

"Did you know this Terrence person? You know, the one that was beheaded."

"Child molester," Buddy spat. "He was the one taking the kids, if you ask me."

The officer eyed him. "You sure about that, Buddy? How do you know?"

"I ain't got no proof, but I was working on it. It's just a feeling, like an intuition or something."

"Alright." The officer wrote a few things down and smiled at him. "Anything else to add?"

"Nope. That's my statement, but I know you ain't gonna use it. You're just gonna come up with some made-up excuse that's believable to the public, aren't you?"

"Yup," said the boyish officer. "There will be no magic trees, no body snatchers, and no zombies in our police report. Thanks for your cooperation, Buddy. You go on home now."

The officer walked away and Buddy took a few steps over to the clearing. The fires were all out now, and there were just some smoking bundles of what had either been citizens or monsters. His co-worker, Ralph, was standing on the other side of the clearing smoking a joint with one of the Stoddard boys. He waved and Buddy waved back.

They had already moved the injured people down the trail on golf carts and motorbikes. It was mostly uniformed police left now. They were setting up the crime scene. Buddy knew they had already pinned the burn victims on that escaped murderer, but he didn't think they had any explanation for why half the town turned up in that clearing on graduation night.

The only civilians left were giving statements or waiting for a ride. Buddy didn't want a ride, and he wasn't going down that trail again either. When the body snatcher had died inside him, he felt it scream before it settled down somewhere in his belly. He vaguely remembered watching everything while he was possessed, like the world was a big widescreen movie, but now he couldn't remember what all had happened between the preacher's place and the clearing being on fire.

After he woke up from his trance, or whatever it was, it only took a few minutes before he was puking and staring down at the lifeless, squirming thing that came out of him. The creature was nothing but a big, fat worm, and he had looked around him to see the others staring at their own worms on the ground too.

He recalled looking up from that dying creature and seeing the other faces that were just as confused as him, and beyond them were the monsters. He caught a glimpse of some of their hairy and scaly backs as they moved away from the fiery clearing and disappeared into the woods.

He remembered feeling like he needed to go near the tree trunk and had zigzagged through the maze of burning bodies to reach it. The wood was burning red and there was no longer anything supernatural about it, but just over the flames, deep in the woods, he saw a familiar face peeking at him from behind a tree.

Behind him, Buddy could hear the approach of motorcycles and electric-powered vehicles, and the flashlights were throwing narrow beams of light all over the place. That face peeking out at him was so white, glowing in the darkness, that he didn't need a flashlight to know who those big, open lips belonged to. He had thought it was a dream at first, until one of the beams of light landed directly on her face and he saw the painted, oval mouth of Lucille clearly for an instant before it vanished behind the tree with a squeak.

Before he could take off after her, he heard Ralph yelling for him and remembered the oath he took to protect and serve. The two of them helped put out the fires and gathered civilians for transport down the trail, and he had given his statement to the uniformed youngster. But now, with the crime scene under control, he slipped off through the woods to find his lover.

He got to the tree she had squeaked behind and there was nothing there. He searched for a few minutes, trying to decide whether to look aimlessly or just go home and wait for her to return. Lucille had never left the trailer before, and she had definitely never been this far from home. He just knew she was lost and scared.

She wasn't like the other monsters that had been in the wild all their lives and knew how to live in the shadows. Lucille had never even been in the woods before. She had never stepped in the dirt or been around living things other than Buddy. She was made to stay indoors, and as the sun was coming up, he waded through a thorn bush in search of the helpless thing.

It only took ten minutes before he found her, completely deflated and lying at the base of a tree. Ants crawled over her face, and the branch of a thorn bush stuck out of her belly. Buddy's stomach turned at the sight of his lover all messed up like that. He frantically removed the thorns and carried Lucille away from the ant bed. He spent half an hour picking the insects and thorns off her body. The entire time he stared into her eyes, waiting for them to move, but they just stared blankly past him.

He was too embarrassed to carry her into the clearing and down the trail, too afraid of what the other people would say. Lucille was different, and they just wouldn't understand. Buddy decided to walk toward the lake and see if he could follow it back to the road.

She was so deflated and lifeless that he could have probably folded her up and tucked her under his shirt. Instead, he curled the tiny arms behind his neck and carried her like a lady, with one arm supporting her back and the other underneath where the knees should be.

He kept glancing down to see if there was any life in those flattened eyes, but whatever life she had earlier was gone. The stars were almost gone too. Walking through the brush, he squinted upward and spotted a faint red light that looked like Mars. Buddy desperately longed for her to be a truly living thing again.

Chapter 26

THE BALD-HEADED BOY WAVED from the shores of the lake, as the Professor finally regained control of his body. It was mid-morning and he hadn't been asleep very long before being brought to the lake.

"What do you want?" asked the Professor. "Couldn't you just call me or something instead of using that dog whistle for wizards?"

The Jenkins boy wore a short-sleeved polo tucked into khaki shorts and had a bright red dragon's head tattoo coiled around his neck. There were tiny holes in his face, lips, and ears where the rings and loops had been removed. A sexless mannequin stood on either side of him. They wore no clothes and tilted their plastic faces toward the Professor as he approached.

"I wanted to say goodbye in person," the boy said. "Why are you wearing a top hat?"

The Professor looked confused. He removed the hat and stared at it for a moment. "I'm not sure. I used to wear it sometimes when...when I was—"

"When you thought you were Abraham Lincoln? Well, you won't have a need of that anymore. Those personalities should be gone for good by now. Coming back from the dead can cure you of all kinds of mental and spiritual ailments. Dying over and over again tends to cleanse your soul out pretty good."

The Professor put the hat back on. "I didn't know I had a soul. I thought you took it from me."

"Heavens, no! I can't take away your soul. That would kill you—for good, I mean. It was your mortality that was necessary for the spell, and removing that always has side effects."

The Professor stared at the dummies standing next to the boy. He didn't want to ask what they were, thinking it might offend them.

"So, where's your friend?" he asked. "Where's Reginald, the knight?"

"Right here," the boy said, pointing a finger to the mannequin on his left. "The other one is actually a sea creature named Maggie. They're not really mannequins. It's a Holoflage spell."

The Professor rubbed his aching head and pointed a finger at the boy. "Listen, I want you to answer some questions, and I want them answered in as straight-forward a way as possible. No riddles or nothing like that. I've been confused about pretty much everything that's happened to me, and if you're leaving for good, then this might be the last time I have a chance to ask a wizard any questions."

"Ask away."

The Professor thought carefully for a few moments. "First, why did you camouflage a giant knight as a mannequin?"

"Well, it's not Reginald that needs to be hidden. It's Maggie. She's from an ancient species that is fairly controversial, and apparently is on the Forbidden Summons List. I didn't know that until the other day, and I can't just walk onto campus with a forbidden creature behind me, can I?"

"But your teachers, they're wizards too. So won't they be able to see what the mannequin really is?"

The boy shrugged. "Eventually they might, but I've heard of students slipping spells like this through. There are a lot of students coming in at one time, and this type of spell is pretty advanced, so they might not be looking for it. I just want to get off the ship and onto campus with them, and then I plan on letting Maggie loose. There's a rather large lake nearby, and I figure she can hide out there and not be too far away. She agreed to come, but only if she can be underwater for the duration of the trip. Maggie doesn't like to breathe on land for very long. So I developed a kind of water suit. It's airtight and she is completely submerged. It's kind of like a space suit filled with liquid."

"She's actually in a liquid suit right now?" asked the Professor.

"Yes, but I had to disguise the whole thing to get her on campus. My mother happened to have these two mannequins in the shed behind our trailer, so I performed a Holoflage spell using them since it would look way cooler walking onto campus with two creepy mannequins than two old mattresses. There was a couch and a recliner too, but I chose the mannequins. Before you ask, a Holoflage spell is where I create a holographic image from a real inanimate object, kind of a copy of it, and place the hologram around something else to kind of camouflage it. The hologram appears animated, but it's actually just a projection hiding the real living thing beneath, which in this case are Maggie and Reginald."

"Why couldn't you just have used something smaller, like a remote control or a fork, and stored them in your pocket or something?"

"The template has to be large enough to cover at least a good bit of the living thing for the camouflage to work. Hence why I almost used two mattresses. I wasn't going to hide Reginald, since he's perfectly legal to summon, but I figured it would make for a better first impression to have two of them. I'll bring Reggie out once Maggie gets settled in the lake."

The Professor blew out a deep breath. "Alright, so that kind of explains the mannequins. How about what happened last night? Why were you there, and why didn't you do anything to help?"

"I was asleep. All the creatures at the gathering were under the Lord of Chaos's spell, including Reginald. He cast a drowsy spell on me while I was already sleeping, and kept me out for the duration. It was all part of my spell. You know, the one that required your mortality."

"What spell?" the Professor asked, scratching his head. "I cut open the hooded creature from the inside out. I killed the Death Hood with that chainsaw." The Professor shuddered. "As for last night, it seems to me that Prince's gasoline fire is what took care of Terrence and the thing in the base of that tree, not anything you did. What spell are you talking about?"

The boy grinned and sat down on a chair that magically appeared beneath him. "There are all kinds of spells. That's what I'm going to school for, to learn about them all. Take what I just did, for example. It's called a conjuration. I took a mental object, something that I envisioned in my imagination, something inside of me, and made it a reality. I imagined a chair and then pulled it from up here inside my head to down there on the ground. That's called a conjuring, or an imagining, which is not to be confused with a summoning, which was what happened last night. A summoning is taking something from outside one's self and causing it to move through space and time. Like when I summoned you from your house to the lake, or when the demonic things in Terrence tried to summon forth the Lord of Chaos last night. Both of them are just different levels and types of summoning."

"Alright, so who started all this? Who summoned the thing that possessed Terrence and got the whole mess going in the first place?"

The boy sighed. "That, I think I can answer. I've conjured up quite a few creatures over the years, but none of them were strong enough to do what occurred in the woods. No, it takes a powerful wizard to summon forth something evil like the thing in Terrence and all its minions that took over the town. I was asleep most of last night, but I remember awakening to see the blazing fires. As Reginald carried me away, I saw the maroon-cloaked man staring back through the trees. It was a face that I hadn't seen since I was five years old, but recognized it all the same.

"The last time I saw my father, he was carrying a coffin into the woods. He liked to sleep in a wooden coffin out in the wilderness, so I didn't think anything of it when he waved goodbye that evening all those years ago. Neither did my mother. Both of us expected him home the next morning, but he never came back. Mom later told me that he went insane before he left, babbling spells that she never understood. Just before she disappeared, she was babbling incoherent stuff too.

"It was my father's face last night, but that face in the cloak had been twisted and mangled through the years, and there was no love in those eyes. There was only an emptiness that validated all the things my dreams had told me about him. There were nightmares with that face in it, but I never thought I would see it in my waking life again. Did you know my father was a history professor? He taught ancient history at the four-year college in town long ago, before I was born. Mom said he resigned, but I think he was fired. In the photo albums at the trailer, there are pictures of both my parents when they were young at parties and social events. Every Halloween party photo had my dad dressed up like an Egyptian pharaoh or a Sumerian deity.

"Anyway, the nightmares got worse when Mom disappeared, but I still never expected my father to be alive, much less behind all this.

It was a few months ago when Mother told me she was going to the grocery store, but I saw her through the window entering the woods, dragging that coffin with her. After a couple hours, I decided to go look for her, and I found the coffin, but I never found my mother."

"I don't know what to say." The Professor bit his lower lip. He was never good at consoling others, but he tried anyway. He was still a boy, for God's sake, no matter how grown up he acted. "I'm sorry for your loss. My parents died when I was young too."

"Thanks, but I don't feel like I've lost anything much. My mother may have taught me some things about magic through the years, but she never loved me as much as she loved my father. And she may still be alive, for all I know. Maybe my parents are finally together and happy again. Whether she's still living or not, I now know that my father isn't dead, though somebody needs to kill him. I definitely won't get that honor, since I'm going out west. I believe my dad was the one that started all this though. I think he conjured an acolyte of Apep, and it got into Terrence. The acolyte was likely an ancient priest mage, or at least the spirit of one. I think Mom heard the wizard call of her husband, and that's why she left. She may be out here too, somewhere, still helping the old man do rotten things. I don't really miss my parents. I have Reginald and Maggie now...and you. You're my friend, aren't you?"

The Professor shrugged uncomfortably. "Why, of course I'm your friend. You're going to write me, I hope."

He knew he would think of more questions once the boy was gone. He could use another friend too, especially another wizard, since he had no clue about how to be one himself.

"I'll email you every week." The boy grinned and then snapped his fingers. "I almost forgot to tell you. The university dean is aware of what went on here last night and she is supposed to let the magical authorities know what happened. You may see some people or things in suits wandering around here in the next few weeks looking for my father, but I don't care if they find him or not. I'm starting a new life today, and those woods are not coming with me."

Albert adjusted his top hat and thought of more questions. "So, your father may have started all this, but that still doesn't explain what you needed my mortality for."

"Oh!" The boy snapped his fingers again. "I forgot to explain the logistics, the process, the meat and bones of how magic works. I may have mentioned it briefly the first time we met, about how a spell is a setting into motion of a chain of events. For example, a simple conjuration begins with a set of instructions that is inserted into the known universe and, once followed, leads to certain end results. It's similar to how coding works, but us wizards can code these instructions down into the marrow of reality. So, Charlie's death, Prince's arrest and subsequent heroism, your many deaths...all these things were set into motion. They were all different aspects of the same spell. The spell that resulted in stopping Terrence and destroying the Priest of the Dark Pit would not have worked without all the various actions and events that led to those eventualities.

"Your mortality was taken and, as a consequence, you played an integral part in both results. Prince's life was altered in such a way as to lead him to that spot in the woods last night. There is a lot of randomness in the world, so there are always some unexpected twists and turns along the path of any real magic. However, a good wizard begins the spell and then makes alterations as it weaves itself through the fabric of the universe."

"So how many spells are out there controlling events in the world?" The Professor rubbed his eyes. "Is everything in this world part of some spell?"

"That's very possible. God could be the most powerful magician in the universe or something. There are wizard mythologies out there that are interesting. I'll send you a book on it if you want. There are too many spells to count in this world, with many forgotten and left to aimlessly weave through the years. Most of them fizzle out eventually, but some keep going long after the creator is gone."

The boy paused and rubbed his chin. "Think of it this way. When you decided to find that little girl's brother, you began a spell. When a teenager decides to go to college, to be a doctor or an athlete, whether they reach these goals or not, the journey is a spell of their own creation. However, most people don't have as much control over their own desires and actions, much less have any influence over the desires and motivations of other humans, much less nature itself. When I cast a spell, it is only a future that I seek to craft this reality into. I create a future reality where the end result is more likely to occur than not, which is something that successful non-wizards can sometimes manage to do without using any actual magic at all."

"So you knew I would kill that creature," the Professor said, "and you predicted that the chain of events leading to last night would likely occur from that death. All you needed to do was take my mortality."

"And other things, like putting a protective cloak over you and some of your friends." The boy stood up as the chair evaporated. "I had to ensure that none of you got possessed by one of those disgusting worm things." The boy took a few steps toward the lake and his mannequins followed. "But there will be no such protection from me anymore. You must find a way to protect yourself for now on."

"From your father, you mean?" Albert asked.

"No." The boy stared at the sky over the water. "Even for such a maniacally evil person as my father has become, this last summoning attempt took a lot of energy. And with police and investigators swarming the place, he will likely hide away for a while. No, it's the non-humans that you'll have to deal with in the near future. Things like the Kraken in the lake, the giant birds, and all the things that crept out of the darkness last night. They all made their way from whatever hiding place they had found to come to these woods...to come to the call of Apep. Sure, most of them turned around and went right back where they came from, but not all. Many are still lingering here and could try to make this area their home."

"What happens if one of those monsters attacks the people around here? Are you saying I should stop them or something? That's what the police are for."

"The police won't always be able to solve your problems," the Jenkins boy said. "I've left behind a few friends that can help you should you need them, but remember that you are no normal human being. You're an immortal wizard now, and as you learn more about yourself, your natural abilities should develop on their own."

The Professor opened his mouth to speak, but was interrupted by the sudden appearance of a monstrous airship hovering over the lake. The huge bullet-shaped air sac towered over a deck where an old, grey-bearded man in a bathrobe and a pointy, star-riddled hat stood waving his hand. Behind him, hundreds of children ran back and forth on the deck, playing and talking loudly. The huge ship creaked and groaned as it swayed above the lake.

"That's my ride," the boy turned to face the Professor. "If you want to know more about magic, you should read some books. There are many out there, and there's a bunch of online videos and informational websites too. I'll email you a list of stuff to read and maybe even send you some books."

"All of those children are wizards? Who's that old man waving his arm?"

"Oh, that's the mascot. He's supposed to be Merlin, but they put a bathrobe on him for some reason."

Something was moving toward them from the deck of the airship. As it got closer, the Professor could see that it was a plank of wood large enough to drive a car onto. The plank extended out slowly, finally coming to rest against the shoreline a few feet away from the boy. Jenkins and his companions stepped onto the wooden board and walked a little ways before turning around.

"If you could send me an email with some books or something," the Professor said, becoming flustered at losing the only other wizard he had ever met, "just to provide some kind of guidance. I would really appreciate that. It's all so new to me. I just don't know where to begin."

"Magic comes naturally once you are aware of it, but it does take a lot of practice to improve. Kind of like your death spell, if you want to call it that. You had to die dozens of times before you finally got the hang of how to use it."

The Professor nodded. "I guess you're right."

"Of course I'm right," the boy said, waving his arm, "and you can always go to school one day, if you want. They let adults in too, you know. Well, goodbye then. Sorry for all the trouble I caused. Hopefully any children I left behind won't be too much of a bother."

The Professor waved back as the platform withdrew toward the ship, taking the child and his mannequins with him.

"Goodbye, Jenkins boy," he whispered to himself. "I don't even know your first name."

He watched the plank retract itself fully back into the airship and could make out the mass of children disappearing into a hole on the deck. He saw the mascot pointing at one of the mannequins and arguing with the boy. Then there was a whoosh of air filling the balloons as the dirigible roared upward into the sky. In the blink of his eye, the Professor no longer saw a ship. It had vanished.

He squinted and put a hand over his eyes, but no matter how hard he looked, there wasn't any ship.

There was a splash in the lake and he turned to see a dozen or so gigantic monsters with fish faces and scaly, humanoid bodies standing in the shallow part. He blinked, and they were gone too.

The Professor turned around in a full circle on the rocky shore of the lake, but couldn't find the creatures anywhere.

Had they been there at all, or had he only imagined them?

He took a deep breath and peered upward, but the black spot in the sky was still gone.

Was I going crazy?

Maybe.

Maybe it was time to embrace the fact that he was a crazy person in a crazy place. Maybe it was going to take a person just crazy enough to believe in things like magic and vanishing airships to defeat things that made no logical sense and did not belong in this world.

He walked through the trees toward the car parked on the side of the road at the end of the trail. There was a loud trilling sound and the splashing of water behind him, but the Professor didn't turn around. He just kept on walking.

Out of the corner of his eye, an ape-like face peered from behind a tree, but he didn't turn his head. Even when he passed by and heard the creature's heavy breathing, the Professor didn't stop until he reached the road. He had no desire to see more monsters. He had seen enough for now and just wanted to get home.

He got into Billy's car and sat in the air conditioning for a moment or two, until the curiosity was just too much. Albert glanced through the window toward where the creature's face had been. It was still there, staring back at him for a few seconds until retreating behind the large tree.

"Bigfoots, I can handle," said the Professor, turning the key and pulling onto the road. "The barn could use another rug."

Prince sat on the floor next to the Professor's recliner, listening to the voicemails play in the adjoining room.

BEEP

"Hello, yes, my name is Ronnie Gibson and I'm calling from Hope Springs and, well, I don't know how to leave a message about it. I saw your card at the Pumping Station and thought I would call. What's going on is I got a garden, see...a pretty good-sized one...and I grow stuff in it, you know...beans, carrots, sometimes squash, and hopefully I'll have some watermelons to pick. Anyway, something has been getting in and eating everything. What I mean is, something is sucking the stuff into the dirt, not pulling it out. It's not a deer or rabbit. It's nothing like that. I thought about a gopher at first, but the other day I seen it and it wasn't natural. Something had its head sticking out of the ground and was eating a carrot. The thing looked almost like a person. It had a human being's head, except for the horns and the fact that it was orange, like a pumpkinhead or something, and—"

BEEP

"Yeah, it's Ronnie again. As I was saying, there's something weird in my garden, so if you could call me at 355-4289, I'd appreciate it. Thanks."

BEEP

"Bob Young here, I called earlier about the goblin thing in my basement. It just asked me a riddle and I didn't answer. Should I answer it or wait until you guys can get here? I called the police, but the creature hides when they come in the house, so now the cops think I'm crazy. So call me back if you want my business, you got my number already. Just hurry up, the thing looks hungry."

BEEP

The messages went on and on.

A little old lady had a werewolf in her shed.

Bill Taylor's dead wife wouldn't leave him alone at night.

A guy named Bubba tried to run over a baby troll in his truck and wanted someone to pay him a visit at the hospital.

There were more than a dozen messages played by the Professor before he unlocked the door and fell into his chair.

"The barn's been empty for a couple days," Prince said. "Where have you been?"

The Professor closed his eyes. "I went into town and got a hotel room. My mother is buried in Memorial Cemetery; my sister too. I hadn't seen them in a while, so... Where's Billy?"

"He's been gone the whole time too. I think he's with Beulah. I heard him come in after the forest fire and he left with her. That was two days ago. The same morning you left with your eyes rolled back in your skull, looking like a zombie or something."

"Well," began the Professor, eyes still closed and rocking slightly in the recliner, "when he gets back, we got a lot of clients to call."

He opened his eyes and smiled at Prince. "Have you been watching the news?"

"Yeah. I'm like the most wanted man in America right now. Even the possessed people are saying I caused it all. They're looking for an escaped murderer that led all of them out into the woods and started slaughtering everyone before setting the woods on fire. I'll never leave this room."

"I've been thinking about that," said the Professor. "There's a cellar underneath this floor that's never been used as far as I know. The only entrance is a door in the back yard. If we can cover that door with grass and camouflage it from sight, then we may be able to build an entrance in this floor. That way you could have your own room down there and fix it up how you wanted. Maybe it would give you some extra space since it won't be safe to leave here for a while."

"Maybe I can put a bathtub down there," Prince said. "Professor, I know you told me a little about being a wizard and all, about hearing the voices and everything. Charlie used to hear voices too. It was some woman that spoke to him. Does that mean he was a wizard too?"

"Don't know. This magic stuff is all new to me, but I think it's time I learned more about it. That Jenkins boy is supposed to be emailing me some stuff."

"Can you teach me too?" Prince got excited.

"I don't see why not." The Professor smiled at him from the chair.

"I've read a bunch of fiction books about magic," Prince said. "I wonder how accurate they are."

"How do wizards and witches cast spells in those books?"

Prince shrugged before answering. "It depends. Some stories have different magic systems or ways that magic is performed. One book might explain it as just using your mind or some inner force to make things happen around you. While another magic system might involve transferring energy about or using chemicals and potions. The writers are kind of all over the place. It's fiction, so they're just making it all up. There is no one correct way really."

"I see," the Professor began. "Well, the way Jenkins seemed to explain it is a setting into motion of things. Like, you plan or weave a spell by coming up with how to get from one way of things in time to another and influencing the world around us to get there. Sounds kind of difficult if you ask me."

"Yeah," Prince said, "but how can you use a crystal ball or fly in the clouds that way? Coming up with a plan and executing it doesn't sound like the type of magic I read in books. How do you throw a fireball or raise the dead like that?"

The Professor shrugged. "Don't know. The boy also said he was using his mind to make imaginary things a reality. Pulling them from his mind to the real world. So, I guess he would think about a fireball and then pull it into this world. Maybe there's different ways to do magic too. Jenkins' way may not be the only way."

"That could be true." Prince said. "Your method has been to use your death as a weapon. I guess it's a setting into motion spell kind of thing, but you don't always know the end result. You're not weaving a plan, are you?"

"No." The Professor shook his head. "I don't know what I'm doing half the time. Maybe there are different types of sorcery, but either way, I should probably find out."

"Could you apply to the school?" asked Prince.

"Maybe, but I'm probably too old to go back to school again."

"Nonsense! If there's one thing you're good at, Professor, it's going to school. Just look at them." Prince pointed to the nine diplomas up on the wall. "There's just space enough for a tenth one if you ask me."

"Well, maybe one day. For now, it seems that whatever possessed Terrence and the others summoned quite a few nasty things to this area. The Jenkins boy warned me before leaving that some of the creatures might stick around. We need to be ready for them, try to figure out ways to kill the monsters or otherwise get them safely away from our clients. I got a feeling we're gonna be busy for a while."

Chapter 27

KATRINA SAT ON THE couch drinking a soda as the Professor turned down the television. It had been several days since graduation, and this was the first time she had been back to the barn since that night. Billy and Beulah were on the couch with Kat, and Will sat on Daisy's lap in the chair. Billy was drunk and fidgeting in his seat.

"Alright." The Professor stood by the TV holding a wad of cash. "I wanted to get everyone together to pay you your share. We found Dirt Dobber and the little boy, so here you go." He handed Kat, Daisy, and Will some money. "And Billy already got his share."

Billy grunted and took a swig straight from his liquor bottle.

"Now, I know all of us are really worried about Cris," the Professor began, "and there's not a lot I can say really. He's still technically missing and may still be alive, for all we know."

"He ain't alive!" yelled Billy.

The drunk got up and stormed out of the barn. Beulah ran after him with tears on her cheeks.

The Professor scratched his head and Katrina put her drink on the coffee table. She was ready to go home, and she didn't want to step foot in that stupid barn ever again.

"Is that it?" Kat asked.

The Professor sighed. "No, that ain't it. I wanted to let you know that we've been getting lots of phone calls the past week for jobs, people wanting to pay us a lot of money to solve their paranormal problems. Well, mostly paranormal. Some aren't paranormal at all. The point is, I need some help doing all these jobs. I can't be everywhere, and there's more work than I can handle. Daisy, wouldn't you and Will like to earn some extra cash?"

Daisy nodded. "Sure, why not? You good with that, baby?"

Will got off her lap and sat on the couch next to Katrina. He put his hand on her shoulder. "Kat, are you alright with this? I mean…"

"Yeah." Katrina smiled and touched his hand. "I'm not going to, but you guys go ahead."

Will turned and nodded to Daisy.

"Great," the Professor said uncomfortably. "Let me fill you in on some of the cases. There's this baby troll on the loose and I'm having a problem finding the damned thing. I know they like to hide underneath bridges, but I don't know of any bridges anywhere near here other than Myers Bridge, and I've already been over there ten times."

"Well, I don't know the names of them," Daisy said, "but I can take you to at least four other bridges I know about near here. How big is this troll anyway?"

"Not sure," the Professor said. "I haven't seen it yet, but the man said it was as tall as his truck and as wide as—"

"Professor," Katrina interrupted, getting up to leave. "I think I'm going home. You let me know if you need any more of those business cards. My mom's got the template and everything."

"I will, Kat," he said, stepping forward and hugging her tightly. "You go home and forget all about trolls and things like that. Aren't you getting ready to leave in a few weeks anyway?"

Katrina came out of the hug and faced the Professor. "Yeah. I'm gonna go ahead and start the summer semester. My parents got me a dorm room, but I'll come back during the breaks and see everyone.

Maybe you guys will be rich by then, with all the weird stuff going on around here."

"And we're throwing you a party before you go, whether you like it or not," Daisy said from her chair. "I'll come by tomorrow, alright?"

Katrina waved goodbye and walked out of the barn. Buddy was standing in the middle of the road looking up at the night sky in amazement. She looked upward to see what he was staring at. The sky was unusually clear and full of stars, but she didn't see any planes, or meteors, or anything out of the ordinary.

"What you looking at, Buddy?" she asked, jogging toward the shirtless man in jean shorts and a SECURITY hat.

He looked down at her and took a bite of his brownie. "Hey, Kat. Have you never looked at the stars before? Aren't they beautiful?"

Buddy put the remainder of the desert in his mouth and turned his head upward again.

Katrina hit him in the shoulder lightly with her fist. "Hey! They may be beautiful, but you can't stand in the middle of the road and look at them. Some drunk will run you over in their pickup truck and not even stop to wipe you off the tires. One of those Stoddard boys is likely to come barreling through here on a beer run any minute."

She led him by the elbow off the road and into the front yard of the barn.

Buddy smiled. "How are you doing, Kat? I mean, about the whole Cris thing?"

"You mean him dying? Well, I'm not doing too good, Buddy. It's been less than a week! How the hell do you think I'm doing?"

"Sorry. I'm real sorry, Kat. I was just trying to be nice, that's all. Is there anything I can do? Me and Ralph, we've been worried sick trying to think of some way to help, but every time I approach Billy, he shakes his fist and walks away all mad." Buddy looked up at the sky again as he continued. "I talked to Lucille about it too, but she didn't know either."

"Oh, Buddy. You are a moron, aren't you?" Kat sighed and looked upward in the general direction that he was staring. "Are you looking at anything in particular, or just staring at all of 'em?"

Buddy pointed. "Right there. That's what I'm looking at now. It's called Orion's Belt. See those three stars grouped together, and the arms going out from the top and the legs below? The three stars are like the belt and everything."

"Hey," Katrina squinted. "I think I see it. Those three little stars sure do twinkle a lot."

"Yeah, they do." Buddy shrugged. "That's really the only one I know other than the dippers, but I like to make up my own sometimes. Right there." He pointed again. "Do you see that triangle up there? I call that one Giza. You know, after the pyramids and all."

"I think I can see it. How's Lucille been doing anyway?"

Katrina had never actually seen Buddy's girlfriend, and she didn't know anyone that had. She imagined her as a slow, beastly woman who never left the couch.

Buddy put his arm down, but kept looking up. "Doing pretty good. We got engaged, you know. Going to get married in a few weeks. I got a honeymoon planned and everything."

"Really? Can I come?"

"No. Nobody's coming. We're having a private ceremony with just the two of us and Ralph. Ralph's gonna marry us. He's a minister, you know. Got his certificate and everything."

Katrina touched his arm. "I'm really happy for you, Buddy. Lucille's a lucky woman."

Buddy turned and smiled, but then shook his head and looked right past her. "Poor Billy."

Kat turned to see Billy passed out against the side of the barn with the liquor bottle still in one hand.

Buddy scratched a hairy belly button and shook his head. "Kat, I'll tell you one thing. Don't you ever get so sad about nothing that you go and disappear from life like that. I know you're sad about Cris and all, but I'm pretty sure he would be like most people and want you to go on living and not be drunk and sad all the time like Billy. I mean, I'm sure there are some mean people that would want their loved ones to grieve like he's doing after they're gone, but I don't think Cris was like that. I don't think he had a selfish bone in his entire body."

Katrina wiped the tears from her eyes and hugged Buddy so hard that when she was done, she pulled two chest hairs off her cheeks.

"Since when did you get so smart, Buddy? Naming constellations and giving out good advice." Kat eyed him suspiciously. "Come to think of it, you're calmer than I've ever seen you before. Who are you and what did you do with Buddy?"

"I'm right here." he looked around to make sure no one could hear, and then leaned in to whisper. "When I asked Lucille to marry me, she said she would, but only under one condition. I had to see a doctor about my brain problems. She said I was getting too paranoid about everyone. So I went and they gave me a prescription for some brownies. I do feel a lot calmer, but I don't want anyone knowing that I'm taking anything. Can you keep a secret, Kat?"

"Those are pot brownies?" she asked.

Buddy shushed her. "Now, don't you go telling anyone, especially not Daisy or those barn friends of yours. They'll tell Beulah and she'll blabber it to everybody. No, this has got to be our little secret. Just me, you, and Lucille. Got it?"

"Got it," Katrina said, and they shook hands.

"Good." Buddy nodded. "Now let's get Billy's ass in bed. It's supposed to rain later."

Together they put one Billy arm around each of their necks and carried the drunk into his house. Beulah woke up and threw a bucket of cold water on her boyfriend's head and that got him alert enough to stumble into the bedroom with her.

Kat left Buddy staring at the stars and walked through the trailer park where she had spent her entire childhood. She crept past the eerily empty Jenkins house, then walked briskly by the Stoddard trailer. Their dog, Bitch, was snoring in the driveway and paid no attention to her as she passed. No one was on the porch, but she could hear the loud party going on inside, and Katrina knew how unpredictable drunk people could be. The last thing she wanted was to be spotted by a drunk Stoddard with the sun down.

When she got home, everyone was in bed and all the lights were off in the trailer. She silently turned the doorknob and tiptoed to her bedroom. Kat took out a jazz record and put it on low volume before getting on her pajamas and settling underneath the sheets. Thanks to Buddy, she got in her bed that night feeling less guilty about being alive than she had all week.

The girl lay in the bed with the lights off for close to an hour, listening to the jazz record play with her eyes closed. She had slept with Cris's skin suit every night, but for some reason she didn't feel like getting up to retrieve it at the moment. Besides, it had been a risky thing to do since her parents might wake her up in the morning and find it, so it was probably best to keep it hidden while she slept for now.

The needle ticked to the last track and it was one of her favorites. A live version of "Body and Soul" played in the darkness and the sound of Dexter Gordon's saxophone brought a smile to her face. She was on her side nestling into the mattress with eyes closed when she heard a rustling noise just outside her window.

Her eyelids opened, and for a brief moment she glimpsed two gigantic eyes staring back at her through the glass, before they darted out of view and there was only the back of the trailer next door. Something about those eyes had been so familiar…but they couldn't be. Whatever had been watching her had to be a giant, since her window was a good eight feet off the ground. She hadn't gotten a good look at the face, but from just a glimpse she knew it had to be a monster.

Katrina lay in shock for a moment or two before rushing out of bed and through the trailer. She suddenly knew where she recognized those two huge eyeballs from and remembered the creature that had protected her in the woods, the fish-faced thing that had gazed at her with love in its eyes.

Kat opened the trailer door and quietly closed it behind her. She stepped down the stairs and around the side of the mobile home, turning the corner, but she found nothing at her window.

The night was quiet…too quiet.

There were no insects making noises and no dogs barking. The muffled jazz saxophone could be heard through the closed window of her bedroom. The girl looked around one last time and, seeing no one else in the darkness, she spoke, not knowing why she chose to say what she said. It just felt right.

"Cris? Is that you, Cris?"

She heard footsteps and a huge, monstrous head peered out from behind the far corner of the mobile home. The oversized, lidless eyeballs stared at her from across the back of the trailer. The thing was waiting on her, waiting for her to say or do something.

"Cris?" Kat asked again.

The enormous monster took another step out into the open and the girl carefully stepped closer to it, inch by inch, as the saxophone continued to play behind her window.

Katrina crept closer and closer until she was near enough to wince at the foul-smelling breath. She reached out her hand and gently touched a scaly cheek. Kat nodded and let the tears flow as the creature pressed its cheek against her fingers and the fish lips gently kissed the palm of her hand.

Chapter 28

THE MAN CALLED THE Professor sat in the recliner and read the email from his laptop:

Dear Albert Miller,

At this time, we cannot accept your application to the West Coast Wizard Academy. We are sorry, really sorry about this. It really tears us up to have to say no. It's just that you don't know anything about wizardry, nothing at all really, and you have to have some basic knowledge to take even the most novice classes that we offer. Why don't you take a few years and try to learn more about yourself first? Maybe you can find a mentor where you live? You can always re-apply later if you want. We understand that you didn't know what you were until very recently, and that is not unusual. We have some older students that found out late in life, but they, too, had to learn a few things on their own before ever stepping foot on our campus. Once again, we are sorry, and hope you will not give up on the avocation of wizardry.

Yours Truly,
DEAN SMITTERKINS
A KIND-HEARTED WIZARD
OFFICE OF ADMISSIONS
THE WEST COAST WIZARD ACADEMY

He clicked on the Inbox and opened another email, one that he had read several times already:

Albert,

I got your last email and sent a few links below to websites that might be helpful. There's also a list of textbooks you can buy online that might help too. I hope your application gets accepted, but if not, don't worry about it. You can apply again and again. I had to apply three times before I finally got in. I hope your human friends are doing alright, and from what I've seen on the news you've been pretty busy dealing with the mess I left behind. Hope you're making lots of money.

As for your questions, the Bigfoot and the fish men will not harm you. They are your friends. That's probably why you've seen them lurking around a lot. I asked them to keep an eye on you before I left.

Anyway, keep studying and learning and I'll try to come back and visit during the Christmas break. It's good to hear from you, Albert. Feel free to keep up the questions or send me a message if you just want to talk or something. By the way, good job with that little troll. As my Living Things teacher says, the only good troll is a dead troll!

P.S. Have you checked the house lately?

Your Friend,

JENKINS

He closed the laptop and set it down on the coffee table. Albert rocked back in the recliner and put his feet up. He closed his eyes and felt the weight of all the deaths and rebirths that had occurred in that chair.

Had it been over a thousand by now?

When he lifted his eyelids, nothing in the room had changed, but it took a moment to realize that he had not died, that he had only closed his eyes.

For a while, he hadn't liked closing his eyes in the chair at all, but now he found that there was something comforting about that recliner. Sometimes Albert actually liked to be reminded of how it felt to wake with a gasp and feel the life flooding into his body. It was only a snap of the fingers, the time it took his consciousness to go from the blackness and emptiness of death to the feel of the cushion in the darkness, and then the blurred vision of the little room and the gasping breath. It would be too easy to chase that feeling of re-birth over and over again until the earth collided with the sun, or maybe longer than that.

Would I live forever?

Albert knew he could outlive the recliner at least. Prince had helped him run some tests to find out more about the condition. The most recent tests were to determine if the chair had anything at all to do with the phenomena. It didn't, of course. They took the chair out of the room, and he just woke up with a gasp and fell the two or three feet to the floor where the furniture had been. A bruised tailbone had taught them that he would always re-materialize in that very spot, whether there were four walls and a floor there or not. It only took a couple of tests before they put the chair back in exactly the same spot as it was before and invested in a new seat cushion.

He stood and lifted the hairy rug off the floor. Then he opened the cellar door and descended the steps. At the bottom, he waved at Prince, who was sitting at a writing desk reading by lamplight.

"Billy's gone now," Albert said. "You can come up if you want."

"I might," Prince said, putting his book down on the desk. "To be honest, I kind of like it down here now."

Albert had to admit that the room was cozy. The concrete floor had been covered with rugs of all sorts. The whole area had been set up years ago as a kind of bomb shelter, in case of an alien invasion or nuclear holocaust or some other stupid thing that Billy had been afraid of. There was a smell of lavender and vanilla, probably from one of those candles Prince liked to light sometimes. Despite being underground, the little man had kept the room very clean. There were two mattresses stacked up in one corner, with the writing desk and office chair in the other. In the middle of the room were two kitchen chairs to sit on, but they never sat on them. Most of the time, Prince would just come upstairs and sit on the rug if they wanted to talk.

"You doing good for books?" asked Albert. "I can get you some more from the library."

"I'm good for now. Is Billy gonna be gone long? Is it a good time to get a bath?"

"I think so. He's gone to Beulah's and they usually stay over there to do their drinking nowadays. Why don't you come on up?"

Prince grabbed some clothes from a gym bag and followed Albert up the stairs. They left the room, and the dainty man took a long bath while the wizard made them some sandwiches. It was already dark outside and he figured Billy wouldn't be back until the next morning. Albert locked the barn door just in case, though.

Prince had become one of the most recognizable faces in the country, a regular old Charlie Manson according to the media. Unless they had been living under a rock that summer, anyone that walked in that barn and laid eyes on Prince would instantly recognize him as the deadliest man in America.

Albert had mostly been working the jobs alone. Kat was already finishing up her summer college courses and Billy was too drunk most of the time to hold a conversation, much less work. He would get some help from Daisy and Will occasionally when there was muscle required, but it had mostly just been him and Prince trying to outsmart some creature or another, usually culminating in Albert going somewhere and killing himself in the process. They had collected more money that summer than he knew what to do with. As the cash piled up, he just put his head down and plugged away at the torrent of jobs that never seemed to stop.

"I like the cameras you set up," Prince said, emerging from the bathroom with steam still rising from his skin, freshly dressed in pajama bottoms and a bright purple tank top. "I watched you talk to that new client yesterday, which saves you having to explain it to me all over again."

"They were pretty cheap," Albert said, pointing to the tiny, barely visible camera at one corner of the ceiling. "Spying is easy these days."

Prince sat down on the couch and Albert brought over two plates of sandwiches.

"Thanks," Prince said, taking a big bite and talking with his mouthful. "You feeling better today? About not getting in and everything?"

"Yeah," Albert said after he finished chewing. "I'll just apply again in another year or two. Jenkins sent me some books to study, and I've looked at a few of them already."

"Learn anything yet?"

"Well," Albert said, holding up his half-eaten sandwich. "Watch this."

He whispered some silent words, closed his eyes, and furrowed his brow.

"Meow," came a feline voice from behind Albert's secret door.

Prince giggled as he ate the sandwich. "That's the third cat you've conjured up by accident. What were you trying to do anyway?"

Albert studied the sandwich. "I was trying to make the tuna disappear from between the bread, but it's still there and now we have another damned cat."

Prince slapped him on the arm. "You'll get better, man. I tell you what, instead of giving this one to Beulah, why don't we keep it? I could use some company down in that cellar while you're out working."

"Meow."

"What if it *meows* while Billy's here and he goes looking for it and finds you?" asked Albert, who never really liked cats to begin with.

"Listen, I've got to have something other than the books. I know there's some risk, but maybe we can create a soundproof area down there or something. You've got a lot of money now, don't you?"

"I could just tell people it's in my room. No one goes in there but you anyway. How about you just promise me to be careful and I'll consider it. Alright?" Albert took a bite of his sandwich.

"Meow."

"It's hungry," Prince said, holding the last bite of his sandwich and standing up. "I'm going to feed it. You coming, Albert?"

"No. You go feed your cat. I'm going to stay out here for a minute. Make sure and close that door good behind you."

Prince walked into the room with KEEP OUT on the front of it and closed the door behind him.

Albert Miller finished his sandwich and stared at the television, furrowing his brow, closing his eyes, and trying to focus all his thoughts on the electrical currents, the microchips, to force his will on an inanimate thing, going through all the steps described by Magus Willard Yancey in the treatise on...

"Meow."

"Meow."

"You need to get some cat food," yelled Prince from the other room.

Albert grimaced and took the plates into the kitchen before opening the front door of the barn and stepping outside. The sun was down and Buddy was standing in the middle of the road.

"Get in the grass, you idiot!" Albert yelled.

Buddy looked down from the sky and stepped into the front yard.

"Sorry," Buddy said, waving his hand. "I get to star gazing and forget myself."

"I know," Albert said, closing the door and walking over toward him. "We all know. You've already been hit by one car. You've got to be more careful, Buddy."

"I know Prof—" Buddy began, "I mean, Albert. I know it's dangerous. There's just less light pollution here, with Billy's house and the barn not being lit up and all. How's Billy doing?"

"Drunk. He's always drunk. You know that."

"I know," Buddy said, looking back up at the stars. "Just trying to make conversation is all. I'll get better about calling you by your new name too. It'll just take some time."

"It's not a new name. It's the one I was born with," Albert said, turning to leave. "Just stay on the goddamned grass, will you?"

"Sure thing, Albert."

He stopped at the barn door, the barn that he had called home all these years. Albert touched the old piece of wood and turned around at the sound of tires on gravel to watch a huge monster of a truck barrel down the road. With its window up, he could still hear the country radio station inside. The driver honked and Buddy waved at them without taking his eyes off the sky.

The truck disappeared up the road and Albert wondered how many of the people in this park, or in this entire town even, believed half the things they had been seeing the last several months. All those people out there driving around in their trucks, many of them were even at the clearing on the night of the big fire, and almost every single one of them refused to believe in things they call the supernatural, even things they may have seen with their own two eyes.

Take the man who hired Albert to find that troll, for example. Even when he was face to face with the dead creature held up in front of him, the man had just shrugged his shoulders and said it was probably a fake. The insurance company had said so too, but they hadn't denied his claim.

But the troll was real, no matter how badly that man didn't want to believe it. That kind of innocent refusal to face strange and scary new facts would have frustrated the Professor or whatever personality he had undertaken at the time, but not Albert.

He watched Buddy standing in the darkness and looking up. The wizard named Albert closed his eyes, focusing hard on the sky above. He concentrated on the darkness behind his eyelids, and then all the elements of a shooting star, finally envisioning a fiery rock flashing across the early evening sky.

"Did you see that?" asked Billy.

"It wasn't a cat, was it?"

"A cat?"

"Goodnight, Buddy," Albert said, opening his eyes to see the man still looking upward and excitedly bouncing from foot to foot in the grass.

Smiling, the wizard went into the barn and left his neighbor in the yard waiting for another star to shoot across the sky.

About the author

Stephen Rhoades is the author of the novels *The California Butcher* and *Rat Droppings*. His stories have been included in the horror anthologies *Inanimate Things: Volume One & Volume Two*. He currently lives in the darkest parts of Alabama with his wife and family.

Get access to exclusive updates on Stephen Rhoades at www.butt inchair.com.

9 781967 519019